About the Author

Victor Nicolle has been writing for film and television for more than twenty years. Mr. Nicolle has received several writing awards, including an A.C.T. Best Writing for Children's Television, a Leo Award, and the 2020 Daryl Duke Prize for Screenwriting. He lives in Vancouver, British Columbia.

The Remarkable Adventures of Thrasher and Wren

Victor Nicolle

The Remarkable Adventures of
Thrasher and Wren

Vanguard Press

VANGUARD PAPERBACK

© Copyright 2024
Victor Nicolle

The right of Victor Nicolle to be identified as author of
this work has been asserted by him in accordance with the
Copyright, Designs and Patents Act 1988.

All Rights Reserved

No reproduction, copy or transmission of this publication
may be made without written permission.
No paragraph of this publication may be reproduced,
copied or transmitted save with the written permission of the
publisher, or in accordance with the provisions
of the Copyright Act 1956 (as amended).

Any person who commits any unauthorised act in relation to
this publication may be liable to criminal
prosecution and civil claims for damages.

A CIP catalogue record for this title is
available from the British Library.

ISBN 978 1 83794 136 0

This is a work of fiction. Names, characters, businesses, places, events and
incidents are either the product of the author's imagination or used in a
fictitious manner. Any resemblance to actual persons, living or dead, or actual
events is purely coincidental.

Vanguard Press is an imprint of
Pegasus Elliot Mackenzie Publishers Ltd.
www.pegasuspublishers.com

First Published in 2024

Vanguard Press
Sheraton House Castle Park
Cambridge England

Printed & Bound in Great Britain

To my parents, my children, and Sandy.

Chapter One

A Tale of Two Losers

Before I start telling you my story, I'd better introduce myself. My name is Roy Archibald Thrasher. I know, it's kind of a funny-sounding name, especially the Thrasher part. My mom said it was originally spelled T-H-R-E-S-H-E-R, which was the same name as these giant machines with rotating blades that they used to use on the prairies to cut down wheat and bundle it all up. Maybe they still use them, I don't know.

But the point is, when my great-grandfather came over here from Europe, he didn't want to use his real name, so he just made one up from the first thing he saw at the immigration office, which happened to be a farming magazine with a picture of a threshing machine on it. Lucky for me, it wasn't a gardening magazine or I would have ended up with a name like "tulip" or "daffodil".

Whenever I mention my name, people think that I was named after these birds called Thrashers but that's not true. I've never had anything to do with birds. Well, that's not entirely true either. In fact, I've had a lot to do with birds lately, as you'll see. But I'm getting ahead of myself.

As far as being a kid goes, I'm what adults would call an under-achiever. My average mark last year was C minus. Which isn't bad considering that both of my brothers failed grade five and I never did. Somehow, my sister ended up with all of the brains in the family. She made it onto the honor roll in high school and was voted most likely to succeed, although they never said at what. I think if you added up all the brains from my two brothers, my sister and me, you'd end up with one regular-sized brain. Or maybe a brain and a half. You see? I can't even figure that out.

As for popularity at school, I'm pretty much at the bottom of the pecking order. Which is funny considering that the name of the school I go to is called Hummingbird Elementary School. Get it? Bottom of the pecking order? Hummingbird Elementary? Okay, so it's not the best joke in the world. And it's not even mine, to be honest. But at least I'm trying. And my school really is called Hummingbird Elementary. So there.

The next part of this story has to do with the fact that it's not all just about me. It's also about this girl named Judy. I've known Judy since kindergarten but we never really talked to each other. I pass her by in the hallway all the time and never say anything to her. And she never says anything to me either. We just kind of nod and turn away and ignore each other or grunt. I think we ignore each other because we both know what we are. There's a name for it, and it starts with the letter 'L'. See if you can guess what it is.

There's this unwritten rule that says losers don't talk to losers. Although, now that I've written it down, I guess that's all changed. Anyway, Judy Edna Wren, that's her full name by the way, came from a poor family. Even poorer than my family and that's saying a lot. Her father seemed to be out of work all the time. And I heard that her mother used to add this powdery stuff and a ton of water to their milk just so Judy and her two sisters had enough to drink.

She never looked poor. I mean, her clothes weren't ragged or anything. But you could tell they didn't have a lot of money. And she always looked sort of sad. Like I say, losers don't talk to losers. And a lot of this information is second hand from other kids. But that's how adults get most of their information, right, so what's the difference?

You're probably wondering why I refer to myself as a loser. I mean, think about it. What else could be your conclusion, given the following? Fact number one: no one has ever mistaken me for handsome. Fact number two: I have two flat feet and an equal number of knocked knees. Fact number three: because of fact number two, I'm the slowest runner at school by a long shot. Fact number four: due to facts number two and three, and the fact that I'm scrawny, I always get picked last when it comes to team sports at school. Fact number five: because of facts numbered one through four, plus the fact that I have acne and bad breath which I can't seem to get rid of no matter what I do, I've never had a girlfriend.

Whenever I ask a girl at school to dance, which is almost never, she usually says something like, "Um, I'd really like to but I'm not feeling well," and then she walks away and starts giggling to her girlfriends. Fact number six: there are so many more facts on this 'loser list' that I can't even be bothered naming them all.

Don't get me wrong. It's not like I've given up. I read this book once that said Thomas Edison tried a thousand times before coming up with the stuff that made his light bulb work. Well, I've probably tried nine hundred and ninety-nine times to get girls to like me and it hasn't worked yet, so I must be getting close.

Last summer, I sat down and took a hard look at my life. Since I wasn't smart or fast, or good looking, I thought maybe I could be tough. Or at least act tough. This friend of mine, Leonard, said that I should form a gang because I had the perfect name for it: "Thrasher". So, I took his suggestion and formed this gang called The Thrashers that had me and Leonard and two other guys in it. I was supposed to be the leader of the gang but the other guys wouldn't listen to me.

After two months, they held this secret meeting and had a vote and then they demanded that I pay five dollars to attend my own gang meetings. I refused, mostly because I didn't have the money, but also because it just didn't seem right. Why should I have to pay to attend my own gang meetings?

I got up the courage to join the lacrosse team at school but that only lasted two weeks. I couldn't remember any of the plays and the first time I got hit I thought I was going to die.

I tried out for the school musical earlier this year, "Bye Bye, Birdie", but the teacher said I was tone deaf and that it wasn't fair to the other students so she let me go.

I've had three part time jobs in two years and lost them all because I supposedly kept saying the wrong things all the time to the customers. What's wrong with saying, "Why, Mrs So And So, you look so much more lovely now than you did last week!" or "Mr Jones, I really like your hair cut, did you do it yourself?" If you can figure out what's wrong with saying things like that, you let me know.

That girl I was telling you about, Judy Wren, she has her own list of loser qualities which are probably longer than mine. In grade three, she had to get glasses, these big plastic ones that made her eyes look like a bug. In grade four, she placed dead last in the school spelling B. I remember that clearly because the one who placed second to last was me. In grade five, she tried out for the school cheerleading squad and was told she was too plain. I never thought she was plain. But then who am I to talk? And I certainly would never tell her that. I would never say she wasn't plain either. She might think I was attracted to her. And then what would happen?

Anyway, Judy and I continued on like this, all the way through kindergarten and elementary school, pretending the other person didn't exist. It just seemed easier that way.

And then, one day, from right out of the blue, something happened that changed our lives forever. Actually, it wasn't just one thing that happened, it was several. And it all began with the arrival of this really weird looking substitute teacher by the name of Mr Crane.

Chapter 2

Mr Crane

None of the students remember Mr Crane arriving at school. He didn't come by car or bicycle, so we just assumed he took the bus or walked. I mean, that's how most teachers got to school. But Mr Crane was so tall and stooped that we didn't think he'd be able to bend far enough down to even get onto the bus, let alone sit in one of the seats. So, we figured he must have walked to school. And given the length of his legs, and the distance that each of his steps covered, it probably wouldn't have taken him long, even if he was coming from Timbuktu.

Mr Crane was already in the classroom sitting at his desk when we arrived. Judy isn't in my homeroom class so she doesn't remember seeing him, but I do. He was super thin and his head had the funniest shape, long and pointy, with tiny black eyes and a tuft of hair that stuck up from the back of his head like a broom. When I got there, he was eating something out of a plastic bag. I thought maybe it was rolled oats or sesame seeds or something. Only he wasn't using his hands to eat it. He was jabbing his pointy mouth right down into the bag and then arching his head back so the food would slide down his throat.

I mean, I've seen strange eaters before. Corey Pickford, this weird kid from South Africa, used to eat the banana peels and throw away the fruit part. My friend Leonard used to nibble around the edges of his sandwich and lick the filling off before throwing the rest of the bread away. I mean, we all have strange habits. But nothing, and I mean, nothing, compares to the first time I saw Mr Crane eat his snack.

Students aren't dumb. They know when there's a substitute teacher that you can get away with almost anything because substitute teachers don't know who you are, and most of the time, they don't care. They're only there for a couple of days and then they're off to some other school, never to be heard from again. But Mr Crane was different. He watched everything and everyone. His dark little eyes would scour the room constantly looking for who knows what. Once, Leonard and I saw him watch this beetle crawl slowly across the floor. His attention did not waver for even an instant. At one point, he got so excited that we thought he was going to leap up and pounce on it, but he never did.

After a few days, we got used to Mr Crane. Me and Leonard would spot him at lunch sitting by himself near the school pond. He'd make this throaty sound when he swallowed his food. And then, after eating, he'd wander around the pond, stopping now and then to stare down into the water. A couple of times, I remember him standing on one leg for what seemed like forever. I thought maybe he had a sore foot or something, but I don't think so because I saw him later walking around normally as if nothing was going on. Anyway, there's no point going on about how unusual Mr Crane looked. It's what he did that mattered.

As I said, I'm not the smartest kid in school. And as I also said, substitute teachers are known for not caring about the class they're teaching because they won't be there very long. So, when I found out Mr Crane was going to give us a math quiz that our regular teacher, Mrs Algonquin, had forgotten to give us, it seemed like the perfect opportunity to, you know, cheat.

Now, don't get me wrong, I almost never cheat. And when I do it's just so my math grade won't drop below a 'C' minus. If it goes below a 'C' minus, my mom freaks out and has to hire a tutor and that eats into my video game time. So, it's a risk that I'm willing to take from time to time. And I was willing to take it this time. With Mr Crane. Even though I knew he had these beady little eyes that seemed to see everything. So, what was I thinking? I don't know. And believe me, if I had to do it all again, I wouldn't. But I did. And I wished I hadn't.

So, you're probably wondering what happened. Well, let me tell you, it wasn't pleasant. I bought the answers to the math quiz for two dollars from Zack, this guy that I know who is a year older than me in Grade 7. He said Mrs Algonquin always gives the same math quiz every year, so I thought I had it made in the shade. I had the formula questions stuffed in my jean pocket and the multiple-choice answers written down on the palm of my hand, you know, 1-D, 2-C, etcetera. I was wearing these gloves that my grandmother knitted for me last Christmas to cover them up. I pretended I was really cold in the classroom and that was why I was wearing these gloves. Everybody else seemed to fall for it. And I was pretty certain by the time I'd gotten to the end of the exam that Mr Crane had fallen for it as well.

Well, guess what? Just as I put my pencil down and was starting to feel really good about things, I noticed that Mr Crane wasn't sitting behind his desk at the front of the room any more. In fact, I couldn't see him anywhere. And then I noticed that everybody in the room was suddenly quiet. And they were all looking at me. I turned slowly around. And there was Mr Crane, standing on one leg, right behind me. He'd been watching me for who knows how long. He reached over my shoulder, and with those long arms and bony fingers of his, pulled off my grandma's gloves. I felt a river of sweat run down the sides of my forehead.

I had a choice, he said. I could come with him to the principal's office immediately and probably be expelled from school forever. Or I could serve a two-hour detention in his classroom after school. I chose the detention of course. I mean, who wouldn't? Little did I know that no matter what I chose, it was going to change my life forever.

Chapter 3

The Detention

I wasn't the only one who got a detention from Mr Crane that day. Judy also got one, although I didn't know it at the time. During morning recess, Mr Crane caught Judy littering on the school grounds. It didn't matter that the type of litter in question was an apple core. Or that it was organic. Or that it was actually good for the environment. These were all things that Judy pointed out to Mr Crane, but it didn't make any difference; he was going to give her a detention no matter what.

Now, like I said, I didn't know Judy very well at the time. But I did know her well enough to know that she's not the kind of person who goes around littering for no reason at all. And when Judy told me later that she hadn't littered, and that she was only setting her apple core down on the bike rack for a few seconds while she tied her shoelaces, I believed her. I also believed her when she said that a great injustice had been done to her. Maybe it was a bit over the top saying it like that, I mean, she wasn't going to jail or anything, but I got the point. Justice is justice and injustice is… well… it's just not right. And Judy getting a detention for setting an apple core down on a bike rack for a couple of minutes was definitely an injustice.

There wasn't anybody else that got detentions that day. Just the two of us. And it was Mr Crane who gave them both out. So, Judy and I figured he must have got up on the wrong side of the bed, or whatever he sleeps on, and that she and I, being the losers that we were, just ended up paying for it.

By three-thirty in the afternoon, almost everyone, students and teachers, had left for the day. There were a few kids playing soccer outside. And you could hear, down the hall, some of the drama students rehearsing songs for the upcoming premiere of "Bye Bye Birdie". I wasn't bitter that it wasn't me singing those songs but I wasn't happy about it either. I've learned to accept that some people can sing well and others can't. And that nobody is going to pay five dollars to listen to somebody who can't sing. I mean, I wouldn't, so why should they?

I think the worst thing about the detention was seeing how scared Judy was. I don't think she'd ever had a detention before. At least it looked like she hadn't. Her forehead was wrinkled and her eyebrows made her face look worried. And she kept twisting the ends of her hair around into this rope thing and then letting it go until it was straight again.

Mr Crane had us both sitting up next to each other at the front of the class. There's this big clock above the blackboard and I remember trying to get the second hand to move faster by using the power of my brain but it didn't work. The second hand actually seemed to slow down the more I tried to make it speed up. I'm sure scientists have an explanation for this phenomenon, but I just chalk it up to being frustrated when you really want something that's right in front of you to change and it won't.

By four o'clock, Judy and I started glancing over at each other. That 'L' word started popping up in my brain. Hers too, probably. Here we were, two losers stuck with this weird teacher who seemed to be half asleep with his eyes open, staring at us in silence, and there was no way out.

At four-fifteen, Mr Crane opened his lunchbox and pulled out a container full of brown squirmy things. They might have been gummies but I'm not sure. He picked up a couple of them and tossed them into his mouth and swallowed them without chewing. Then let out a burp. Judy and I both tried not to laugh. But I think we giggled loud enough to catch his attention. He closed his lunchbox and glared at us. Judy and I were petrified.

Mr Crane cleared his throat. It sounded horrible. "Do each of you know what you did wrong?"

Judy looked at me. She didn't know what to say, so I jumped in. I nodded to Mr Crane.

"Yes, sir. I got caught cheating on my math exam."

"That's right," Mr Crane said. "What about you, young lady? What did you do wrong?"

Judy swallowed hard. "I put my apple core down on the bike rack?"

Mr Crane shook his head. "You littered, missy. And there is no excuse for that."

Judy nodded. "Yes, sir."

Mr Crane made us promise to be better students in the future. At that point, Judy and I would have said pretty much anything. So, promising to be better students wasn't much of a stretch. But then Mr Crane said something strange. He asked us how we could make the world a better place because pretty soon it would be too late for us.

I remember scratching my head and looking at Judy. Too late for us for what? Before I could get up the nerve to ask him what he meant, Mr Crane had opened a metal container of what looked like berries and uncooked fish. If there's one thing I've learned about living with adults, you don't want to interrupt them when they're eating. So, I let it go, hoping Mr Crane would let us go home early. But he didn't.

By four-thirty, everyone else who had been at school had gone home. One of the janitors walked by in the hallway pushing a giant broom. He glanced at Judy and me and gave us both a raised eyebrow. I mean, what's that supposed to mean? A raised eyebrow? He doesn't even know us. Does he think we deserve everything we got? I mean, maybe I do. I'll admit that. But Judy doesn't. And where does he get off thinking he's better than us? Pushing a broom? Anybody can do that. Even my two brothers.

As I sat there, I could feel my anger growing. A couple of times I thought about causing a distraction and then running out the door. But I didn't want to leave Judy behind. Who knows what Mr Crane would do? He'd probably triple her detention and then she wouldn't get out of there until midnight or something. Can you imagine spending an entire day and night in detention? You might as well be in prison, which, when you think about it, is what it is anyway.

I tried to settle myself down. I looked over at Judy. Her body was slouched down and her head was lowered. I think she was trying to nod off. Mr Crane was staring right at her. I'm pretty sure he was getting ready to come over and shout at her or caw, or whatever he does when he's angry, when she sat up suddenly.

Sometime later, I glanced out the window. I saw a couple of kids playing soccer at the far end of the field. I looked up at the sky and could see two seagulls circling high above the field. I remember wishing I could be one of them. Then I could fly out of this classroom and soar high about the earth!

It was nearly five o'clock. Mr Crane seemed agitated. He arched his head back and looked up at the clock. He cleared his throat to get our attention. "I'm going to the washroom. When I come back you two may leave. Do you understand?" Judy and I nodded. Mr Crane got to his feet, accidentally knocking over his chair. Judy and I snickered again but managed to control ourselves. Mr Crane picked up his chair and then made his way awkwardly out through the classroom door and down the hallway.

Fifteen minutes went by. I had to say something. I turned toward Judy. "Where is he? He said he was just going to the washroom."

Judy shrugged. "What do you think we should do?"

I told her I thought we should leave. Judy shook her head. No way. "Maybe he's sick or something. Or fell in the toilet. I mean, what was that weird stuff he was eating?"

The way I saw it, if we left and got caught, we'd be in big trouble. But if we stayed and did nothing we could starve to death. Or worse, Mr Crane could be injured or lying dead in the washroom and we might get blamed for not helping him.

Suddenly, at the back of the room, there was this giant WHAM! that caused both Judy and I to jump out of our seats. Judy looked at me. "What was that?"

I was sure something had hit the window. We both raced to the back of the room. Some feathers and gooey stuff were stuck to one of the windows. We looked outside. On the ground below, was a mangy looking bird with grey/blue feathers that was struggling to get up onto its feet.

"We have to do something," Judy said, "before a cat comes along and finishes it off."

I looked over at the clock. It was five-twenty-five. Mr Crane had been gone for more than a half hour. That did it. I told Judy we were going to help that bird out no matter what. She smiled.

"Yes," she said, "Nobody is going to blame us for doing that!" We grabbed our stuff, tore out of the classroom, and raced down the hall.

Chapter 4

The Bluebird of Happiness

On the school grounds, beneath the classroom window, we found the bird. It wasn't small, but it wasn't big either. It was still trying to stand up and it was staggering around in a circle like it was dizzy or drunk or something. When it comes to the animal world, Judy is a lot braver than me. Probably because I never had much to do with animals when I was growing up. My dad never let us have any dogs or cats. We had a snake once and two turtles named Rock and Spike but they only lasted a week. And we had this rabbit named Chris that my uncle found under a car on Christmas day. But nothing you could really call a pet or take for a walk.

Anyway, Judy wasn't afraid of the bird, so she picked it up and looked at it. The bird seemed fine but then what do I know? Some of its feathers were torn off and it had this weird look on its face, almost like a smirk, but then who can tell by looking at a bird's beak what it's thinking.

The strange thing was that this bird had a piece of paper rolled up and stuffed into one of its claws. Judy pried open the claw and unrolled the piece of paper. She tried to read it but her glasses were dirty, so she handed it to me. The piece of paper said: "May the bluebird of happiness grant your wishes!"

We looked at each other. Judy frowned. "Too bad it's a blackbird," she said. I couldn't tell a pigeon from an ostrich so I took her word for it. As far as I was concerned the bird didn't look black or blue; it looked like a bunch of different colors. Somebody was obviously playing a joke. I looked around to see if there was anybody recording us with a camera but there wasn't anyone in sight. I asked Judy how she knew it was a blackbird. Turns out she used to go with her dad to the park and feed the birds when he was out of work. She said it made him feel better. Looking at this bird, I could see why.

Just then, the bluebird, I mean, blackbird, whatever, got scared and started to move around a lot. Then it got this burst of energy and flew out of Judy's hand and into the sky. Judy and I watched in amazement as it fluttered around for a bit and then disappeared up into some trees. Judy and I smiled at each other. And then I realized something. After all these years we had finally said more than two words to each other. Wow.

Then came the awkward part. There was no way I was going to go back into that school again. Who knew what Mr Crane had in store for us? And I wasn't sure where Judy lived. But I did know it was in the opposite direction from my house. So, we just stood there. Nodding uncomfortably to each other. And then we turned around and left.

By the time I got home, it was getting dark out. Dinner was ready and my parents were wondering where I'd been. Since I'd already cheated on an exam and got caught and suffered the worst detention in the history of the world, I thought telling one more lie couldn't hurt. So, I said I'd stayed at school in order to try out for the chess club. I don't think my father even heard what I said, but my mother gave me a look that said 'You, play chess? Give me a break!" I think they'd been so disappointed in me for so long that they didn't care. Neither of them asked whether I got in or not, so there you go.

Anyway, during dinner, all I could think about was how horrible Mr Crane and that detention was and how incredible it was to have connected with Judy after all these years. She was not at all what I thought she'd be like. I thought she'd be mousy and kind of dumb and silly and then would talk my head off when she got the chance. But when it came down to it, and here's the weird part, she was a lot like me.

All through the rest of evening, my mind kept wandering back to Judy and how she didn't seem completely unattractive to me any more. Let me put that another way. I used to hate the way she looked: her straight brown hair, her plastic glasses, the kinds of dresses she used to wear. They always seemed old fashioned to me. But now, when I think about her, I think her hair looks kind of cool. It's this golden-brown color. And the way it hangs down over her shoulders is very interesting. It's not like any of the other girls. As for the glasses, I know they're plastic and everything, but when I imagine her without them, she actually looks pretty.

As I was watching TV with my brothers, they had no idea what I was thinking about. And if they ever got wind that I was thinking about a girl, especially someone ordinary and 'plain' like Judy, they'd never let me live it down. That's the great thing about thinking, nobody knows what you're up to. Because if they did, people would be fighting all the time. As it stands now, they only fight half the time. So that's a good thing.

When I got ready for bed that night, I was feeling kind of strange. There was a major storm outside with wind and rain. I looked at myself in the mirror as I brushed my teeth. I still had a lot of acne on my chin and nose and forehead, and my teeth were this dark yellow. The color of old bananas. I worried what Judy must have thought. So, I brushed extra hard and I washed my face a couple of times. I've heard people say that you only make a first impression once. I never knew what that meant. But I must have made the same impression on Judy about a million times over the years. And maybe that's why she never talked to me up until now. Who knows?

By the time I got into bed, I must have been shiny due to all the brushing and washing that I'd done. It's probably the cleanest I've ever been, except, of course, for when I was a baby, but I don't think Judy would have been interested in me back then.

I turned the light off and just laid there, thinking about the day. For most of my life, nothing had happened. The days all seemed to be the same. And then today came along and now all I can think about is a girl; the same girl I've been passing by in the hallway for years. How does that make sense?

Outside, the wind was blowing and causing a tree branch to scratch against the side of the house. I thought I could see the shadow of a bird fluttering around the window, but it must have been the streetlight casting shadows against the window curtain. No bird is going to fly around in a storm like this. At least no bird that I know.

I looked at the clock on my bedside table. It said midnight. Exactly twelve. Which you hardly ever see. Usually, you'll see three minutes past midnight or two minutes to midnight. As I laid back and stared up at the ceiling, the storm outside got bigger. A flash of lightning startled me. I thought the power might go off but when I looked at the clock it still said twelve. Had it been less than a minute since I last looked? I looked away and counted to ten and looked back again. It was still midnight. So, there you go. That proved it. The power had gone out. But then the clock wouldn't be lit up if the power was out. And it was still brightly lit. And the streetlights were on. And I could see light under the door out in the hallway. I was baffled.

Another flash of lightning. Whatever was going on, I didn't want to be a part of it. If it was the end of the world my parents would take care of it. Or the government. Or some superhero somewhere. Nobody expects a twelve-year-old to do anything. So, I closed my eyes and tried to go to sleep again. I thought as long as I kept them closed, everything would be okay. I'd wake up and take it from there.

As I kept my eyes closed, I remember looking forward to seeing Judy at school the next day. This time I'd talk to her in the hallway. This time we would actually have something to talk about. Judy. I even kind of liked her name. Judy. Judy. I said it to myself a few times in a row. I think I was even muttering it to myself as I fell asleep.

The second I nodded off, a crack of lightning ricocheted off the highest lamppost in the city. It split the lightning bolt in two, sending one part of it through my bedroom window—and another part of it through the bedroom window of a house several blocks away.

For a moment, the two bedrooms were bathed in a brilliant blue light. But that quickly faded and the rooms became dark again. How do I know? Because I kept one eye open through all of it. I hoped that it would be over soon. And it was.

Chapter 5

A Shocking Discovery

The following morning, I opened my eyes. No more storm. No more lightning bolts. Just the ceiling overhead. A little further away somehow. But with the same faded yellow paint. And the same glass ceiling lamp shade with the rose shaped pattern that had always been there.

Was I relieved? For a moment. And then I thought about all that had happened the day before. The detention, Judy being worried, how weird Mr Crane had acted. And then I wondered if Judy was waking up somewhere thinking the same thoughts. Maybe she was thinking about what I was doing. But then I thought, there's no way. People are never thinking about what you think they're thinking about. They're always thinking about something else. She'd probably already forgotten about what had happened.

I turned my head to the side. Something didn't feel right. I could see the old chest of drawers between the closet and the door. But there was something in the way of what I was looking at. Something dark was sticking out between my eyes. I know there's a word for it but I just don't know what it is. Wait a minute. Protuberance. That's it. I guess I knew it all along.

I rolled my head over to face the other side of the room. There it was again. That same dark thing. The protuberance. I could feel that it wasn't just a big clump of hair. It was solid and heavy and a definite part of me. I shook my head back and forth. The protuberance followed. I could not get rid of it. The faster I shook my head, the more I freaked out. And I was able to move my head really fast. What if it was the biggest pimple the world had ever seen and I'd grown it in just one night? Great. Just what I need for the next time I see Judy.

Whatever it was, I had to get rid of it. So, time to get up and go down the hall to the bathroom. But my legs weren't working right. And neither were my arms. In fact, I couldn't even see my arms. When I lifted up what should have been one of my arms, all I could see were feathers. Feathers? Stuck to what? I flapped it around in front of my face. Feathers?

I accidently hit my nose. It felt long and pointy and black. That couldn't be my nose! And my hands. Where were they? And everything else for that matter. I tried to sit up but I couldn't. I raised both of my arms and saw nothing but feathers! I flapped them wildly with great speed and energy. The wind pushed me back against the bed.

I looked back. The pillow behind me seemed huge. Ten times bigger than I remembered. And the window was further away. Was that it or was it something else? Time to check out my feet. Get them moving again, get the blood moving, and then everything would be okay.

I tried lifting my two feet. But saw nothing. Just a couple of bony sticks with thin dark webs and claws on the end. I could move them but so what? Where were my legs and feet? I started flapping my feathery arms around. Was it Halloween? Did I miss something? I jumped up in bed. I just stood there. Balancing. On my fat little body. With my tiny stick legs and my webbed claws. And that giant protuberance between my eyes.

Wakey, wakey. Time to wake up. I'd had enough of this dream. I spun around and nearly fell over. I remembered that my chest of drawers had a mirror on top of it. But I couldn't get up there so how could I see myself? And did I really want to see myself? If I had a giant four-inch zit on my face maybe I didn't want to see it. And yet I had to find out. Especially if I was going to be seeing Judy at school that day.

Whatever my arms had become, I flapped them in desperation. My fat feathery body lifted off the bed. Whoa! What was that? I tried it again. Same thing, only higher this time. Then higher still. Like a trampoline. Only I could stay at the top for as long as I wanted. I floated awkwardly over to the chest of drawers and crash landed on top, falling over onto my side. Great. Not only do I look stupid but I'm still the same spaz I was before. What else could happen? I took a deep breath.

I spun around and gazed straight into the mirror. But I couldn't see myself. In fact, I couldn't see anything.

Except this chubby little bird-faced thing on two legs. I was gone. Replaced by a beak on sticks. Okay, enough of the freak show. Time to bring in the adults. I opened up my beak and called out.

TWEET! TWEET! TWIRLY-TWEET! I tried several times. TWEET! TWEET! TWIRLY-TWEET! Over and over. The same thing. Only not very loud. There was no way Mom or Dad could hear that. TWEET! TWEET! TWIRLY-TWEET! Is that all I knew? Because that's not what my brain was thinking. But that's the only thing that came out. Why? Wasn't it obvious? I was a bird. The evidence was standing right in front of me. Staring back from the mirror.

TWEET! TWEET! TWIRLY-TWEET! Come on. How useless is that! I knew I needed help and I needed it fast. But from whom? And where? And what would they be able to do to help me anyway? I thought about Judy. She's the only one I could talk to. She'd understand. Don't ask me how I knew, I just did. But how do I find her? I don't even know where she lives.

I looked down at the clock radio next to my bed. The time was seven-fifteen a.m. I could hear Mom's hair dryer in the downstairs bathroom. And Dad banging pots and pans around in the kitchen. He was making breakfast. And in a couple of minutes, once he got the water on the stove for porridge, he'd be coming to wake me up. I had to get out. It's okay if they figured that I'd run away or something. But if they saw a bird in my room and figured out it was me, well, I can't imagine what would come next. But I'm sure it would involve a lot of screaming.

At the far end of the dresser was my cellphone. That's it! I'll just call somebody. And say what? TWEET! TWEET! TWIRLY-TWEET? I hopped over to the edge of the dresser and stood over the phone. I could see myself in the black surface of the screen. At the side of the phone was the ON/OFF button. I pecked at it with my beak. The phone switched on. I pecked again at the camera button and the camera turned on. Yes! Now what? I need to leave something, some kind of evidence, as to what happened to me. I pecked at the reverse button and managed to take a selfie. I checked the photo in the gallery. I looked like some giant bulging black-eyed bird face from a carnival somewhere. How perfect for the school annual. Why, I can hear all the mothers now. "I wonder what he plans to be when he grows up?"

I fluttered down off the chest of drawers and onto the window sill. A blind covered most of the window but I could see daylight filtering through. It's times like this when the strangest thoughts run through your mind. I thought about how I could still watch TV because I could use my beak to press the buttons on the remote control. Wouldn't that be wonderful? And whenever Mom wanted to watch Oprah or one of her cooking shows, I'd be able to fly the remote control over to her lickety-split. She'd be the envy of the neighborhood. "Why, Mrs Thrasher, you are so lucky to have a boy like that. But who cleans things up when he poops on the carpet?"

I could hear my dad coming out of the washroom and down the hallway. "Roy, time to get up." He knocked on the door like he always does. At that point, I knew I had five minutes. Five minutes before he'd knock again and then open the door and come in to wake me up. At least he was predictable. But how was that going to help me? I had to get away—and now.

Chapter 6

First Flight

The crack at the bottom of the window couldn't have been more than an inch. I stuck my beak through. I can't believe I'm saying this. My beak. Yes, I have a beak. Don't you have a beak? Well, I do. And I stuck it out through the crack at the bottom of the window. And then I pressed the rest of my head out through the crack, and squeezed by chubby body all the way through until I was standing completely on the outside of the window. Teetering and swaying in the breeze. Gazing down onto the front yard of the neighbor's house. I heard a noise from inside my bedroom. It was my dad knocking at the door again. He was two minutes early.

"Roy, time to get up!" I wanted to answer him but it was impossible. He rapped on the door again. His voice becoming impatient. "Roy?" In one second, he was going to open that door and then he'd wonder where I'd gone. I'd had enough. The last thing I needed was to see was my mom and dad in a panic.

Whatever happened, I wasn't going to be of much use as a bird sitting out on a window ledge. So, I decided to take off. But just because you have wings doesn't mean you can fly. Look at all those inventors that built airplanes that didn't work. They had wings. They'd fall right off a cliff and crash onto the rocks below. So, what was below me?

I stuck my beak out a couple of inches, turned sideways, and looked down. There was a sidewalk directly below my window. Lined with rocks. Concrete and rocks. That should break my fall nicely. A bird like me was given wings for a reason. At least that's what I told myself. At this point, I was ready to believe anything. But I also had a hunch that these wings could support me. And if they didn't, well, like they say in the old movies that my parents watch: "It was nice knowing ya".

Just as I was about to jump, the bedroom door behind me swung open and my dad entered. He looked around. "Roy?" You should have seen his face. Total confusion. Like he was a prison guard and some prisoner he was looking after had vanished into thin air. I felt sorry for him. I really did. How was he going to explain this to my mom. "Gee, Donna, he was there when I tucked him in last night. I guess he decided to move on." Maybe they'd be relieved. Let's face it, I wasn't exactly their pride a joy. But at least they wouldn't have to hire a math tutor for me any more. And Mom wouldn't have to do all the stuff that mom's do. But they'd miss me. Don't you think? They'd have to.

Anyway, I took one last look at my dad's face and prepared to jump. Maybe my parents would have squished bird for dinner. With a little mac and cheese. Pile on some ketchup. There might even be leftovers but I doubt it. At least it would start to make up for all the trouble I'd caused them.

I leaned forward and felt the weight of my tiny body begin to drop. I spread my two wings out. Man, they were long. And wide. No way these things would do anything but collapse. But they surprised me when they caught a gust of wind. I could feel myself rising. I was back up to the height of the window again.

I could see my mom rush into my bedroom. She stood next to my father. Her face became as white as a marshmallow. And then I dropped suddenly. Like a rock. Only I wasn't falling forwards, I was falling backwards this time. How stupid is that? What kind of bird falls backwards and then crashes onto a sidewalk. This kind of bird, if you must know!

But I wasn't ready to die yet. There'd be plenty of time for that later. I spun around in mid-air. Spread my wings wide. And caught another layer of wind just inches before I would have hit the ground. Suddenly, I was soaring along the sidewalk. The concrete was a blur. I was going what felt to me like a hundred miles an hour. Up over the neighbor's fence, above their apple tree, and over the top of their garage.

I glanced back and saw my house becoming smaller and smaller. I spun around, just in time to miss the power transformer on the telephone pole in the back alley. It took a few moments to figure out where I was heading. East toward the school. Along the sidewalk below. The same sidewalk I'd walked along hundreds of times. Only now I could see what lay ahead.

When you're high up you think you can see everything. I say 'think' because there were things that lay ahead of me that I couldn't see. Things that nobody could have seen. And if I had known what they were, I would have turned around and gone home and just spent the rest of my days huddled underneath my parents back porch. But I didn't. I kept going. In the direction of school. I wanted to see Judy. I knew she'd turn up there eventually. She had to. Don't ask me why, but I was pretty sure that whatever had happened to me, she could help.

From fifty feet up and thirty miles an hour, 43rd Avenue looked pretty good. I couldn't see much of the litter on the boulevards. The grass looked tidier. And the houses better kept. Everything looks better when you're fifty feet up in the air. You should try it sometime.

I hung a left where 43rd crosses Sophia Street. It's kind of silly to follow streets when you can fly anywhere. But it's the one sure way I could figure out how to get to the school.

I think part of me was scared at not having access to any of the maps on my cellphone. This was probably the longest I'd gone without checking my phone. What if Judy had called? But then again, where would she have gotten my number? It didn't make sense. Besides, you never know who's listening in to your conversation. What if someone had heard: "I was flying over the school yesterday and I just had to take a dump, so I let one go."

Pardon me. But these are the thoughts that come up when you're soaring above the streets and businesses and houses you've known your whole life. Only now you get to see them from above.

43rd dead ends at Fraser. I angled left and headed up to 41st Avenue and then north toward the school. I'd never realized how big Hummingbird Elementary was. An entire block long with several outbuildings and annexes that fit hundreds of students.

I thought, if Judy were to try and reach me, where would she look? I flew in the direction of the place where we had found the bird that had crashed into the window. There was a set of wooden stairs that fed into the building and I thought I could hang out underneath there until I saw Judy. At least I'd be safe. Nothing could harm me there. Or so I thought.

Chapter 7

I'm Not Alone

When you're a couple of inches tall, everything looks huge. Under those stairs were discarded candy wrappers, an old BIC pen, a piece of moldy gum that looked like a giant slug, and a couple of stinky cigarette butts. Oh, and a partly crushed can of Canada Dry. I could hear footsteps crunching on the gravel nearby. A shadow loomed over the wooden steps. Somebody was arriving at school. Coming in the side entrance. It must have been one of the janitors. Or some nerdy student. Or maybe the lacrosse coach. I remembered that they used to have seven-thirty a.m. practice on weekdays. Or was it six-thirty? What difference did it make. I couldn't tell anyway. I didn't have my watch.

And then I heard another noise. A pecking sound. A few inches away. The discarded Canada Dry can was moving. Was there a mouse inside? I wasn't much bigger than a mouse myself. They don't have beaks. But they have sharp teeth. What if it was really hungry and felt like having a bird for breakfast?

I took a few hops backwards. At this point I was pretty much ready for anything. I had my beak ready. I wasn't going to let some mouse push me around. Then I heard a scratching sound. Some dirt flew over top of the can. Suddenly, the can swerved around on its crumpled base and there was another bird standing there, smaller than me, rounder, with multi-colored feathers. It was shaking. And not because of the cold, because it wasn't cold. No, this bird was shaking because it was afraid.

It stared at me. I think it was as surprised as I was to see another bird. I mean, how many birds normally hang out under these steps? I let loose with a barrage of tweets. TWEET-TWEET TWIRLY TWEET TWEET! TWEETLY-TWEET, CHIRUP, TWEET! CHEET-BEEP TWIRLY CHIRUP! Wow, I didn't know I knew that many words. And what the heck was I saying? I know what I meant to say. "Don't be afraid. Who are you? What is your name? Where do you come from?" And then I added, "I come in peace". I got that from a science fiction movie that I saw once. It seemed appropriate.

What I said seemed to calm the other bird down. It came back at me with a few questions of its own. TWEELUP, CHEEP, FLIC FLIC FLIC, CHEEP. I shouldn't have been able to understand what all that said, but I could. It was, "I live around here. What's your name?" Being the genius that I am, I replied, "Roy". The other bird blinked at me in shock. Then said, "I'm Judy". I must have blinked at her in shock too. I don't remember. But I do remember a lot of things suddenly popped into my head. The storm. The lightning bolt that split into two. My wish that I could turn into a bird and fly out of that detention. And my memory of the weirdest substitute teacher in history.

Judy hopped toward me. Just knowing it was her made me feel so much better. "It was him, wasn't it?" she said. "Mr Crane. He did this to us."

"I don't know if it was him or not," I replied. "Did you make any kind of a wish while we were in detention?"

Judy moved her tiny beak up and down. "I remember wishing that I could be one of those seagulls that were flying around outside. I just wanted to fly away."

I shook my beak in disbelief. "I made the same wish." I hopped around in front of her. I could feel myself getting worked up. "Great! This is just great. As if I didn't have enough problems." I was kicking up a lot of dust. My beak suddenly felt heavy and my feathers made me feel like I was wearing a thick winter coat.

"I wouldn't do that if I were you," Judy said. "People are going to be able to see all that dust and know we're down here. Not only that, but I saw a cat here earlier."

"A cat?" I shouted in a flurry of tweets. "We've gotta get out of here!" Judy told me to calm down. She said she knows the cat. It's just a tiny stray that the girls at school named "Snowball" and everybody feeds her so she's not going to be hungry, and Snowball wouldn't hurt a fly anyway. She just lives in the bushes behind the school.

Hearing that, I breathed a sigh of relief. Then I realized that Judy and I were talking just like we had been before. Even though she was an egg-shaped ball of feathers on two sticks, she was still the same Judy I had been thinking about for days. That was a good thing. Amidst all the other bad things that had happened, that was one good thing. And I shouldn't forget it.

"We shouldn't hang around here," I said. "Snowball can't be the only cat that wanders around the schoolgrounds." Judy agreed. "Do you know how to fly," I asked her. Boy, what a stupid question. As soon as I asked it, I knew I was an idiot.

"Of course," she said. "I got here, didn't I?"

"Yeah, sorry," I said. "I don't know what I was thinking." Judy said it was okay. And that I shouldn't be so hard on myself. We put our beaks together and figured out a plan. We'll fly around to the other side of the school, where the street is, and perch up on one of the telephone wires. We were pretty sure that telephone wires didn't have much electricity flowing through them so we thought it should be safe. Judy was more certain about that than I was, which is kind of embarrassing. I mean, guys are supposed to know that kind of stuff, aren't they? About electricity and tools and everything. But to be honest, I couldn't have told you which was a telephone line. But I had seen birds perch on that particular line before, so it had to be the one. Otherwise, Judy and I would be history. And I wasn't quite ready for that yet.

We made our way up to the telephone lines and sat next to each other. It was hard balancing at first. But I got used to it pretty fast. My tail helped. And I could use the weight of my beak, raising and lowering it, to find my center of balance. It was actually kind of fun, like walking a tightrope, only being pretty good at it right from the start.

I didn't sit too close to Judy because I didn't want to make her feel uncomfortable. "Look down there," she said. "Everyone's coming to school." I looked down. Sure enough, buses were pulling up out front. Kids were climbing out of cars. I could see teachers pulling off the street and into the parking lot off to the side. Everyone was arriving at school and talking and laughing just like always. Everyone except us! I looked over at Judy and she was excited at first. But then I could see that she was kind of sad. We just sat there watching. And then I thought about my parents and what must have been happening at home.

Chapter 8

Trouble at Home

Turns out a few minutes after I left, my parents woke my two brothers up and started asking them questions. Ryan, who is two years older than me, was clueless. Spencer, in Grade 10, was even worse. "Well, he must have said something to one of you," my dad shouted. Ryan shrugged and looked over at Spencer.

"I swear, he never told us anything. We never know what he's doing." Which is kind of true. When you're the youngest in the family, people tend to leave you alone. I guess they have enough things going on in their lives to not be bothered with you. I remember my mother used to say to me, "Just go outside and play." And I'd say, "Where?" And she'd say, "In the sandbox." And I'd say, "But there's cat poop in there." But she didn't care. She just wanted me out of the house. And I don't blame her. She worked hard all the time and having me hanging around didn't help. So, I guess I deserved to play in cat poop.

My brothers thought I must have run away. My mother asked them if I had been seeing a girl. My brothers laughed. They thought that was hysterical. "Roy with a girl. Mom, where have you been?" My dad gave my mom a 'don't be ridiculous' look. Was it really that far-fetched for me to have run off with a girl? I mean, let's face it, that wasn't that far from the truth.

My mother really started to freak out when she went into the bathroom and saw that my toothbrush was still there. "If he was going to run away," she said, "he would have taken his toothbrush!" Which is true. I believe in good dental hygiene, even when on the run.

My brothers and dad searched my entire bedroom. There was nothing. No clues. No evidence linking me to a mysterious international conspiracy involving runaway twelve-year-olds. Even my lucky four-leaf clover was still in its plastic case on my dresser.

My dad found my cellphone and tried to turn it on but he couldn't. He shoved it in Ryan's face. "Here! You're good at this sort of thing." Ryan turned on the cellphone.

"What am I looking for?" Spencer suggested looking for phone calls that had been made in the last few days. There was nothing. I hadn't phoned anyone in over a week.

Ryan gave the phone to Spencer. "What about pictures?" my dad asked. "Doesn't he take pictures of anything?" Spencer flipped through the screen to the gallery page. He turned it on. His jaw dropped. He drew the phone closer to his face. "What the heck?" My mother rushed back into the room.

"What is it? What's going on?"

Everyone gathered around. Spencer turned the phone around to show them. It was that last photo that I'd taken. Of me. With my giant bulging black-eyed bird face.

My dad said, "So what? Who cares if he took a picture of some bird."

To which Spencer replied, "Dad, it's a selfie.".

My father couldn't figure it out. Then he spun around and caught my mother as she fainted.

Chapter 9

Rio and the Art of Worming

Back on the telephone wire, Judy and I could feel our legs getting tired. We'd been staring down at the kids arriving at school, trying to pick out the ones that we knew. None of them were really friends of ours, but it was fun anyway. And then I heard a flapping sound and turned around.

Another bird had landed between Judy and me on the wire. A smaller bird, smaller than both of us, with a tiny black cap on his forehead. "You're too far apart, move closer," he said abruptly in a series of gruff-sounding tweets. "Do you even know what you're doing?"

I have to admit I was taken aback by his tone. I mean, who is this guy telling us where to sit or not to sit on a wire? And who was he anyway?

So, I asked him that exact question. "Who are you?"

"I'm Rio," he said. Judy gave him a funny look.

"Rio? What kind of a name is that?" Rio said it was a regular name for a bird. Like Twitter and Twirp and Cheerio and Cheeseburger. And Roy and Judy. I was dumbfounded. How did he know our names?

"What do you care? Maybe I heard you talking," he said. "Just move closer together before the hawks and the falcons come by. They'll knock you off the wire just to be mean, but they won't do it if you're together."

Rio was a tough little bird, but he also seemed to know a lot about things. We didn't. That's for sure. So, before he took off, Judy said, "Listen, we're kind of new to this. So, we're wondering if you could, you know, teach us a couple of things?"

"Like what?" Rio said. Judy stared at him in silence. She had a worried look as if to say 'everything'.

"Like what to eat," I blurted out. I hadn't had breakfast yet and I'm pretty sure Judy hadn't either. Rio looked at the two of us. He could see the desperation in our faces. He must have wondered what a couple of nincompoops like us were doing flying around when we didn't even know what we were doing. I mean, how did we get this far in life? Good question. I think if we had always been birds and known as little as we did about being birds, we'd have been goners long ago.

For whatever reason, Rio took us under his wing. He knew that, once the last school bell went off and the kids were safely in school, the football field didn't get used for the first hour. And since it had rained a lot last night during the storm, there would be 'easy pickins' all round. I don't know what he meant by that but I was willing to learn. And like I said, I hadn't had breakfast yet so I was feeling pretty hungry.

Once we reached the football field, Rio made us spread out several feet apart. "You don't want to crowd together because then they can tell what you're up to. You want to hop lightly, move around in circles, don't be predictable." Judy and I were baffled. We didn't know what we were doing. Where was the food?

Rio shushed us. He became quiet and motionless. As if he was listening to something. He cocked his head sideways and with one penetrating eye stared down into the grass like he was looking at something. Then WHAM! He jabbed his beak straight down and pulled a giant worm into the air.

"Worm on!" he shouted. The poor creature wriggled and fought, squirming for its life. But it didn't have a chance. Rio tossed it right up into the sunlight and then swallowed it whole as it came tumbling down. He then licked both sides of his beak with that strange pointy tongue that he had.

"Ahh!" Rio said with satisfaction. "Breakfast is my favorite meal of the day!" I looked over at Judy. She was horrified. I have to admit, I sort of felt like throwing up myself. But I tried to put on a brave face.

"Is this your idea of food?" Rio said it wasn't his idea of food. It was food. Full of vitamins and protein and minerals. And pretty darn tasty too if he didn't mind saying.

"You got a problem with worms?" he said. "Look, I hung around outdoor restaurants long enough to see plenty of humans eating spaghetti, so what's the difference?"

Judy shook her head. "I'm never doing that," she declared. "I don't care how hungry I get I'll never eat worms." Rio looked at me as if to say, 'What's with her?' I had to admit I was beginning to have a change of mind. Or maybe it was my stomach talking. But listen, I mean, once you get over the idea that they're worms, Rio was right. In science class, we learned that worms were nutritious and easy to digest and that there were people all over the world right now who were frying them up and eating them in their salads. And that one he just plopped into his mouth, it did look plump and juicy.

I was torn. If I ate a worm, would Judy hate me forever? Would my breath smell like worms and she wouldn't come near me any more? On the other hand, starving to death didn't seem like a good idea either. And if I became too weak to do anything, I couldn't protect her from whatever she needed protecting from. I had to make a choice.

"Okay," I said to Rio. "What am I looking for?" Rio nodded as if he knew I'd come around eventually.

"You're looking for movement, at the base of the grass stems. The worms rise to the surface after it rains because they can't breathe so they wriggle around near the surface, and because they can't see very well, they end up bumping into the grass stems. When you see that, that's your signal. You go for it!"

I looked at Judy. She was glaring at me as if to say, "Don't you dare". But I'd already made up my mind. And I was sticking with it. Survival or worm breath. Which would you choose? I hopped around in a circle, looking for what? I'd forgotten already. Some kind of movement? The field seemed huge. I turned my head sideways and bent lower, using my right eye to peer down deep into a spot where the grass joined the earth. Nothing. No movement. Just stillness.

And then it happened. A tiny blade of grass moved, right down at its base. It moved again. And again. Like a little green flag waving me at it. Rio could tell that I'd spotted something.

"What are you waiting for? A written invitation?"

I pointed my beak directly at the movement, took a deep breath, and WHAM! Jammed it into the ground. I pulled it back up again. To my surprise, that beak of mine, that unwieldy protuberance as liked to call it, was holding a decent-sized worm between its two beak halves.

"Worm on!" I yelled. The poor little creature was helpless, trying desperately to wriggle its way free. Rio shook his head and sighed.

"What are you waiting for? A worm in the beak is worth two in the grass. Swallow it, man!" I did as he said. I tossed the worm up into the air and down it went. The whole thing. All at once. And then I belched. Rio smiled.

"So how come you shout out 'Worm on!' every time you get one?" I asked. Rio shrugged.

"It's tradition," he said. He learned it from watching fishermen. "It's so everybody else stops what they're doing and doesn't get in your way."

I looked over at Judy. She shook her head despondently. I knew that she knew that what I'd done was the only way we were going to survive.

"It was pretty good," I said to her. "A lot tastier than it appears." Judy glared at me.

"I don't need a pep talk. I just need to know, can you still feel it inside your stomach, because if it feels like a worm wriggling around in there, I'm out. I may as well just give up and die."

Rio gave me a look. I knew what I had to do. I gave Judy my most earnest look. "Not at all. Once it's in your stomach, you can't feel a thing. Just the whole grain goodness of a solid nutritional meal."

I don't know why I said whole grain because that wasn't true. It wasn't a grain at all. But she didn't care. She suddenly had this look of resolve. She hopped forward. And if I hadn't seen it with my own two eyes, I wouldn't have believed it. Judy cocked her head slightly. Hesitated for a moment. And then SLAMMED her beak into the ground and pulled up the biggest worm I'd ever seen. Even bigger than Rio's. Rio let out a cry.

"Yee-haw! You are a natural-born wormer!"

Judy shouted, "Worm on!" She swallowed the worm and glared at us defiantly. I was proud of her. Proud that she was willing to change her mind when it was the last thing she wanted to do. And proud just to be with her. I know I've said this before already, but I was starting to really like her now. More than like, actually. I don't know what comes after like, but you get my drift.

The funny thing after Judy ate the worm was watching her stand there waiting to feel something moving in her stomach. Rio said the worms are pretty much toast right after they've been eaten because of the stomach acid that we all had. But Judy stood there anyway. Waiting to feel something. Anything. And then suddenly she let out this huge belch. Just like me. Which surprised her and caused her to giggle. And I'm not sure if I was seeing things, but it looked like she blushed, which was so cute that it made me like her even more!

Rio said, "You guys look like you need all the help you can get. Just follow me around for the rest of the day. You'll catch on." Rio pointed out that birds can't afford to be picky, especially when the weather starts to turn bad like in the fall and winter. And that's exactly what time it was, when the fall is turning into winter, and the air was cold and damp.

"First things first. Berries," he said. "Because there's not always going to be rain to bring out the worms. Berries are your go-to food when things get tough."

We followed Rio beyond the edge of the football field to where the high ground slopes down onto a lumpy area of grass and rocks that end up in a ravine. I'd been to that ravine before, a whole bunch of times, and seen some of the older kids smoking cigarettes and making out. But I've never taken a look at the trees. Or anything else for that matter. I mean, it's just a ravine, right? A place to hang out.

Rio flew into one of the tall trees that were full of these blue-colored berries that were just starting to turn brown.

"These are good," he said, pecking away at them and filling up his cheeks.

"I know what this is," Judy said, pointing at it with her beak, "It's an eastern red cedar. And down below, that's a firethorn, and over there, is a cranberry bush." Rio didn't know their names and he didn't seem to care. "And those over there are crab apple trees," Judy said. Rio didn't look impressed. "Don't you know the names of these things? We've got a book at home with all the names." Rio shook his head.

"Why should I? I only know what's good to eat and when to eat them."

Rio had a point. Maybe it's important for humans to have names for all this stuff, just in case you want to write a book about them or something. But if you're a bird, what difference does it make? Humans have names for everything: trees, bushes, different kinds of grass, shovels, lawnmowers, and you can bet, worms. I bet we have fifty names for worms, but does it really matter?

Judy shrugged it off. She and I started pecking away at the red cedar berries. I followed Rio down to the cranberry bush and tried some of those. My favorite was the crab apples. Rio said you've got to be careful because, later in the year, they can turn bad and give you a stomach ache.

Rio showed us a few more tricks of the trade. Where to store food before the winter comes. How to eat while keeping one eye open for cats. Which restaurants were likely to leave their dumpster lids open after hours. All kinds of stuff.

On one of our trips around town, I found a half-eaten burrito sticking up from inside of a garbage can out at the back of a Mexican restaurant. It was so good that I gorged myself. I couldn't stop eating. But then suddenly, I didn't feel so good and was pretty sure I was going to barf. But I didn't. I kept thinking that Judy wouldn't want to be with someone who barfed all the time. Rio said I should stick with the healthier stuff. Like worms.

Rio also gave us a few tips on flying. He said you've got to know how much energy you have so you don't get caught short. Nothing worse than being five hundred feet off the ground and you run out of energy. Sure, you can always glide to the ground if there's a stiff breeze. But if there's no wind and there's traffic right down below you, you could end up getting squished.

Judy and I took a lot of flights together. Across town. Over parks and hills. Rio figured we were good enough to qualify for 'bird certification'. I didn't know what that meant. Rio confessed that he just made that up. But he did say the one thing we were definitely lacking was long-distance navigation skills. He said he'd be happy to teach us the following day.

"I'll meet you guys here tomorrow, same time," he said. "I'd offer to show you where to sleep but I like to keep that to myself." Judy and I both understood. There are some things in the bird world that are carefully guarded secrets, and where you sleep is definitely one of them. I mean, how often do you see birds sleeping?

Chapter 10

My Lucky Charm

It was about this time that I remembered my good luck charm back home. I'd forgotten it on the chest of drawers when I left suddenly. And if we were going to be flying long distance tomorrow, I really wanted to have it with me. Judy shrugged.

"What kind of good luck charm?" I told her that I'd bought this four-leaf clover from a fortune teller when we were on a family vacation one year. For ten dollars, she said it would bring me good luck for the rest of my life, which seemed like a pretty good deal. The problem was I only had six dollars on me. She said that was good enough and I thought to myself, wow, this charm must be working because I'm already having good luck.

"I feel like I need to get that if we're going to go anywhere."

With Rio gone for his rest, Judy agreed to accompany me back home. She'd never been to my house and she seemed pretty nervous about it. But she could tell it was important to me, so she came along for the ride. I was nervous too. Not because of Judy. But because I had no idea what had happened to everyone after I left. I was about to find out.

With Judy following, I retraced the exact same flight path that I'd taken this morning. I didn't want to get lost. Judy would have thought I was a real tool if I couldn't find my own way home from school. And like I said before, things look a lot different when you're fifty feet off the ground. You can see a lot more, which can be confusing.

As I approached my house, I noticed red and blue lights flickering in the street out front. My heart sank. Things had gotten serious. There was a police car parked in our driveway with its passenger door open. A police officer was sitting in the car filling out some kind of form.

As Judy and I fluttered up to the window outside my bedroom, I could see another police officer standing inside. He was talking to my parents. My mom was sitting on my bed which she'd obviously made just before the cops arrived. She was like that. Always tidying up before anyone came over. I'm pretty sure if she was a police officer, she'd tidy up the crime scene before the photographers arrived and ruin everything. Anyway, I could also see my father leaning against my dresser, his elbow just inches away from my precious four-leaf clover.

Judy and I landed on opposite sides of the windowsill so that we could both hide behind the curtains. We listened as the police officer asked them all kinds of questions. Was I involved in a street gang? Did I have any enemies? Was I the kind of kid that would have a secret life? Well, I could have answered that one. Yeah. Just look out the window and around the corner and you'll see. Was it a secret life? Not really. If anybody had asked, I would have told them everything.

After a while, I began to feel depressed. I wanted to help my parents but there was nothing I could do. And I needed to get my lucky charm back so that things would start to go better. Someone had closed the window and there was no way inside. Judy motioned for me to try tapping on the window.

"What do you have to lose?" she said. I couldn't think of anything. I'd already pretty much lost everything.

I hopped across the sill and stood in the middle. Judy gave me an encouraging look. I took a deep breath. And started tapping. Quietly at first. And then louder and louder. I could see the police officer glancing over. He gave me an irritated look as if I was interrupting his interrogation, which I suppose I was. But if my parents had any idea that I had turned into a bird, they might let me in.

I kept tapping, over and over. Finally, the police officer had heard enough. He walked over and closed both of the blinds. Great. "To serve and protect"? I don't think so. How about, "To frustrate and annoy"?

I heard my mom saying, "What was that?" and the officer replying, "Nothing. Let's finish up. We've got other calls to take care of." I could tell I wasn't going to be a top priority on their list. If only I had that lucky charm.

Judy and I flew down and around the second officer sitting in the car. He was filling out a missing person's report. I could even read my name on the form. Roy

Archibald Thrasher. Twelve years old. If there had been a box that was labelled, Loser Yes or No, I bet I know which one he would have checked.

Judy and I spent a few moments perched on the light on top of the police cruiser. The flashing colors were exciting and it kept my mind from thinking about how bad things had gotten. If only my parents had looked out and seen us, maybe they would have known. Or maybe they would have just seen two goofy-looking birds hanging around a flashing light for no reason. It didn't matter because they never opened the blinds and looked out. And a few minutes later, the police left with nothing but another copy of a missing child report signed by two worried parents.

Judy and I thought we'd better hunker down somewhere for the night and then rejoin Rio in the morning. There was no point going back to the school and risking being attacked by one of the stray cats that lived near the ravine. Since I knew my house so well, heck, I've lived there my whole life, I figured out a nice spot to sleep on a ledge under the overhang of the roof. There was warm air that came out of the furnace vent all night long and there was no way any cat could climb up that high. Even if they did, I'd show them a thing or two. I'd protect Judy with or without my four-leaf lucky charm. Although, if you'd asked me, I'd prefer that I had it.

Chapter 11

Taking Off

The following morning, Judy and I woke up to the sound of a car door slamming. It was my dad on his way to work. He was sales manager for this place that sold lighting supplies for homes and stuff. They were having a hard time competing against the big hardware stores, so he went to work early all the time to get a leg up on the competition, whatever that meant.

As he drove off, I remembered all the times that he let me come with him to the store on Sunday morning. As I hung around waiting for him to finish his paperwork, I'd challenge myself by turning on every single light in the display window and then turning them all off again before he came out. He never caught me once. But watching him drive off made me feel sad. I wanted him to know I was okay. That I hadn't run away. And that, as soon as I could, I'd go with him to the store again on Sunday morning so he wouldn't have to be alone.

Judy and I drank some rainwater that had filled up in one of the eaves troughs of the house. And then we set off for the school again to see Rio. At least he could teach us the rest of what we needed to survive. I mean, who knew how long we'd continue to be birds, or even stay alive for that matter.

When we got to the schoolgrounds, Rio was nowhere to be seen. We checked underneath all of the stairs. We even went down into the ravine and revisited all of Rio's favorite trees. But he wasn't anywhere. Judy and I waited. Maybe he'd slept in. He didn't seem like he was particularly old. If he was a teenager, like we almost were, well, you know what that's like. It's hard to get up.

We waited. And waited. And waited. We flew over to the football field and practiced our worming skills. No sense being hungry. "Worm on!" we called out every time we caught one. But Rio didn't show up. We hoped he hadn't gotten run over by a car or something. Or eaten by a cat. Or maybe he was just tired of helping two losers who couldn't fend for themselves. We didn't know.

Just as we were about to leave, Judy spotted something tiny and white flapping up and down near the telephone wires where we first met Rio. We flew up and landed on the wire. Judy found a piece of paper folded and tucked into a space where the wires rubbed up against the pole. It read: "Sorry. Had to go. Big things are happening. You'll see!" It was signed by Rio. Well, not exactly signed. It was more like a bunch of dirt that had been scratched together to look like his name.

Judy and I turned to each other. Why would he leave like that? What was this big thing he was talking about? "And why would he say, 'you'll see'." Judy wondered.

Was he planning to come back and show us something? Or did he think we were supposed to go somewhere and see for ourselves? We had no idea where to go. Or even what we were looking for.

I'd had enough. If Rio wasn't going to show us how to navigate, then we'd do it ourselves. I was feeling pretty good about things. We knew how to fly, what to eat, what to watch out for.

I said to Judy, "We'll do it ourselves. I've lived here my whole life. How hard can it be? We're in the city. Mountains to the north. Prairies are to the east. I used to go there every summer with my family. We'll figure it out."

Judy was okay with that. I think she had gained a lot of confidence too. Plus, we had each other, don't forget that. Just having one other person with you, to be at your side, can mean all the difference in the world.

I led the way. Not because I'm the guy or anything. But because I'd lived longer in the city than she had. She moved here when she was six whereas I'd been here my whole life. That didn't make any difference, as it turns out. I still managed to screw things up. But I'm getting ahead of myself again.

We headed across the city toward downtown. Man, what a view! You never realize how tall some buildings are until you fly just above their rooftops. There is all kinds of stuff on those roofs that you can't see from below. Elevator shafts, ping pong tables, lawn chairs, dead trees in pots, window cleaners hanging off ropes. I glanced back at Judy from time to time. I think she was as amazed as I was.

We swooped down and out over the harbor, skirting just inches above the water. There were freighters waiting to load and unload. People in kayaks. I even saw the shadow of a seal swimming just under the surface. But there was one thing that I didn't see. And that was other birds. Judy noticed it too.

As we flew side by side, she said, "Where's all the other birds?" For a moment, I thought I saw Rio on the other side of the harbor perched on top of a tree. But when we got closer, I could see that there was nothing there. It must have been a mirage.

We went up and over the north shore mountains and then down into a series of valleys beyond. There wasn't a lot over there. At least not as far as humans are concerned. But we didn't care because I knew how to get back.

"Just turn around and reverse course," I said to myself. But as we swooped down amongst the endless trees and rivers that lay beyond the local mountains, it became harder and harder to figure out which direction we were flying. At one point, we perched on top of two trees, facing each other. I looked around. I have to admit, I wasn't sure where we were any more.

I sat there quietly for a few minutes, which probably tipped Judy off that I was lost. She said, "Don't worry. I think it's this way back." We flew off. But minutes later, after resting again for a while, she became quiet as well. We looked around. The trees were dark. And flying up above them didn't seem to help either. All you could see were trees and more trees in every direction.

I felt awful. And scared. Judy sighed. "What do we do?" I told her this story about what my dad used to say to me. He said if I ever felt like I was getting lost, I should stay put and not go anywhere, and eventually, he'd find me. Judy pointed out that our parents have no idea where we are, or what we are, so they can't come and get us. And staying in one spot isn't going to do us any good either because it's getting dark out, in case I hadn't noticed.

We tried flying in ever-widening circles but that didn't do any good. We could always find each other, but nothing else.

As the sun went down and darkness set in, it started to get cold. In one last desperate push, we flew in one direction for what must have been at least half an hour. Nothing changed. The same black trees that went on forever. And now the stars were coming out.

"That's it!" I said, "We'll navigate using the stars!" Judy got really excited when she heard this. Until she found out that I didn't know how to navigate by the stars. I knew nothing about astronomy. Less than nothing in fact. I used to think that the North Star was a brand of running shoe. Same with her. She thought Andromeda was a perfume. If only we'd paid more attention in class. We were hooped. And we knew it.

Chapter 12

Lost

As the night wore on, the temperature started to plummet. My bird breath was coming out of my beak in tiny puffs. Plus I was shivering. I mean, who ever thought a bird shivered?

Judy and I stuck close together on a branch. If there were cougars or bears around, there's no way they could reach us up there. And if we survived the night, once the sun came up, we'd fly as high as we possibly could, maybe ten thousand feet up and then we'd be able to see which direction to go to get back home.

I looked over at Judy. I could tell she was scared. I tried to cheer her up with one of my patented remarks. "Why, Judy Wren, you look much prettier now than you did this morning." Judy looked at me like I'd lost my mind.

"What's that supposed to mean?" I told her about how I used to lose jobs all the time by saying the wrong thing. "I'm not surprised," she said. "And I'm not some job, by the way."

I knew that, of course. I was just trying to make her feel better. "You ever wonder how we got here?" I asked her. "I mean, all those years we used to walk past each other and never say a word." Judy acknowledged how awkward that was.

"It's not like I didn't want to talk to you," she said. "It's just that we…" She went silent.

"I know," I said. "Losers don't talk to losers."

Judy said it was more like she felt like a loser, not that I was a loser. And who would want to talk to her? I said I'd wanted to talk to her plenty of times, but it just never worked out. There were always a million kids hanging around or everyone was in a hurry to make it to class.

"I used to worry because you looked so sad all the time." Judy said she wasn't sad. She just doesn't show it very well when she's happy. And when she's walking down the hallway at school, she gets self-conscious because everyone else looks so cool and rich.

"You mean, everyone but me," I said. Judy scowled.

"No, not everyone but you. Everyone and you. Your parents are way better off than mine."

I wasn't thinking clearly when I said, "That's like comparing one pile of dirt to another." Judy looked at me like I was an idiot. "Okay. Forget I said that. I just meant my parents are not much better off than yours. Besides, who cares? I know a lot of kids at school who have a lot of money and aren't happy."

Judy asked me to name one. I couldn't. Which kind of brought our conversation to a close. For the longest time, I kept trying to think of someone who had a lot of money and was unhappy. All I could come up with was Brad Pitt. And he seemed happy all the time.

*

Back at my parent's house, there had been a knock at the door. My mother was in the living room. She glanced at her watch. My father opened the door. Two adults stood outside. They had their coats on. My dad could see a car parked in the driveway. It was old and beat up.

"Glen Thrasher?" the man asked. My dad shook his hand.

"Come on in," he said.

My parents had been expecting these people. They all sat down in the living room. Ryan and Spencer joined them a few minutes later. It was a really big deal. Nobody was smiling. My mom offered them some cookies but nobody was hungry.

As you can probably guess by now, the two people were Judy's parents, Mr and Mrs Wren. The police had contacted them and given them my parents phone number and address when they found out that it was two school kids who had disappeared, not just one. It must have really thrown them for a loop. I mean, one kid vanishing is a mystery. But two kids at the same time means there must be some kind of connection. Some kind of a plot that nobody knows anything about. But there really wasn't. It's just that the same thing happened to Judy as happened to me. It was kind of random, actually. Or at least, I thought it was.

"Mr Thrasher," Judy's father said, "Was there anything going on between Roy and our daughter?" Everyone in my family shook their head. "If they were seeing each other," my mother said, "we didn't know about it." Ryan and Spencer chimed in. They said they'd talked to everybody in our home rooms and nobody had seen us even talk to each other, let alone go out. As far as they knew, we were complete strangers to each other.

Mr Wren scratched his head. "It doesn't make any sense," he said. "Two kids who don't know each other, disappearing at exactly the same time?" My mother was worried.

"Unless they were abducted," she said.

"You mean, by aliens?" Ryan blurted out.

My father lost his temper. "No, you idiot! Not by aliens. And turn that thing off!" He was talking to Spencer who was checking his messages on his cellphone.

My dad turned back to my mom. "I don't think they've been abducted. I don't want to jump to conclusions. I just think there's something going on here that we don't know about. Roy is an unusual kid. He spends a lot of time by himself."

He turned toward Mr and Mrs Wren. "They'll show up eventually. Think of all the crazy stuff you did when you were young." Mrs Wren said she never did anything like run away when she was young. Especially with a stranger. Same with my mom. And Mr Wren. Which kind of put the kibosh on what my dad was saying.

"Well, wherever they are, they're going to get a good tongue lashing when they get home!"

Mr Wren thought that wasn't a helpful comment. And the room went silent after that. I don't know which was worse. To have been in the room that night with those people, or to be lost in the freezing cold forest. At least, in the forest, I was with somebody that I liked.

Chapter 13

Old Crow

Half-way through the night, it started to snow. I first noticed it when I woke up and saw all this white stuff on my beak. "Judy," I said, "check it out". Judy woke up. She felt the snow on her beak as well. We both shook it off. All around us was a blanket of white. It covered the trees, the rocks, the entire forest floor, everything. And it had become quiet. More quiet than I'd ever heard in my life. Can you hear quiet? I guess not. There is always something making a noise. Even if it was just my tiny beating heart. Which seemed to be beating awfully fast, by the way.

The snow reflected everything. And the forest went from being really dark to really light. Judy wanted to go back to sleep. But I stayed awake. Looking around. Listening to the sound of the forest. Somewhere in the distance, I thought I could hear a stream. We hadn't had any water in a while, so I figured the first thing that we needed to do in the morning was get something to drink. And then we needed food. How much energy can you get out of a few worms and some berries? I didn't know. But I could feel my stomach aching for something to eat. I must have fallen asleep because, even before I woke up, I heard the most terrible sound coming from nearby.

"Caw-Caw-Caw! Caw-Caw-Caw!" It sounded like a nail being pounded into my head. My eyes opened. I couldn't see anything. Judy was staring at a tree across from us. Hidden in the shadow of the branches was a crow rocking back and forth on his perch. He was beat up and kind of old looking but his feathers were all puffed up and he didn't seem to be bothered at all by the cold. His relentless 'cawing' was driving me nuts.

"What do you want?" I asked. "Why did you wake us up?" The crow leaped from his perch. He swept across the expanse between us and landed right next to Judy. There were bits of half-eaten food in the corners of his mouth and some of his tailfeathers were missing, plus there was a tuft of feathers sticking up on his crown that made him look like he'd just woken up himself.

"You like b-b-b-being cold?" he stammered. Judy and I looked at each other.

"Not particularly," I replied.

"Well, you're acting like you do." I didn't know what he was talking about. And I was so tired and cold at this point that I could barely understand what he was saying.

"You've got to puff yourself up," he said. "You've got all those nice feathers with nothing in between them. How did you figure on getting warm?" Judy told him that we'd been keeping warm by shivering.

"You must be part of that new Generation Zero," he said. Judy looked at me as if to say 'help!'. I'm guessing this crow had just made some kind of a snide remark.

"Look," I said, "don't you have somewhere else to go?" The crow looked down.

He shook his head. "You mean, like your funeral?"

I'd just about had enough of this guy. I mean, he was old and everything and I respect the elderly for all they've been through and all of that.

Before I could say something to him to let him know how I felt, he said, "You keep shivering and you're going to run out of energy. Puff up your feathers. Trap the air inside, so your body doesn't lose all its heat. Watch!"

The old crow gave us a demonstration. He took a deep breath and exhaled, causing his feathers to expand suddenly and capture the air inside. His whole body seemed to double in size.

"I'm half air now, see? Warm air. And I'm not burning through last night's dinner trying to keep the chill away. If you don't use what you've been given, you're going to lose it all."

Judy tried what the crow suggested. She held her breath and then blew out, puffing up her feathers. She looked like a fuzzy balloon with two eyes and a beak. I couldn't stop myself from laughing.

The old crow scowled at me. "Let's see you do it, city boy."

How he knew I was from the city I'll never know. But I was certainly up to the challenge, especially with Judy watching. I held my breath and then blew out really hard. My feathers puffed up. But here's the unfortunate part — I farted at the same time.

"Ooops." I felt like an idiot.

"Don't worry about it," the old crow said. "It happens to everybody."

Judy and I sat there like two hot air balloons. It was amazing. I felt like I was in a sauna. No need for shivering. Or hopping up and down on one leg. And no need for a pillow either. I was a pillow.

Later that day, Old Crow (which turned out to be his actual name, by the way) showed us where the other animals in the forest hang out and how to get some of the food they'd leave behind. Beggars can't be choosers, my mother used to say. Now I know what she was talking about. If times are tough and there's not a lot of berries or worms around, you take what you can get.

We followed Old Crow down to a creek where some bears had been fishing for salmon that day. There were all kinds of fish bones and bits of meat scattered around. These leftovers were too small for them to worry about. But for us, it was a feast.

Over the next few days, Old Crow showed us a lot of places to get food. At the bottom of trees, underneath the bark, there are all kinds of insects crawling around. Caterpillars, beetles, spiders. Never in a million years did I think I would eat a spider, but when you pull back a big chunk of bark and see them all running around and there's hundreds and hundreds of them, well, I couldn't help myself. I know for a fact that, if I was as tiny as them and there was this giant spider tearing off the roof of my house and trying to eat me, I wouldn't have stood a chance. I felt bad eating them all. But Old Crow said that was the way of the world. You can try and deny it, but it's only going to make you unhappy.

At night, Old Crow slept in the tree across from us. His snoring sounded like my dad trying to start his chainsaw on a bad day. Varoom! Hawwwk! Varoom! Hunnnk! I must have laid awake the whole night. I'd look over at Judy but it didn't seem to bother her. Maybe her dad snored at home and she was used to it. Or maybe she just liked the sound of a Husqvarna on its last legs. Wow, I can't believe I remember the name of that thing.

During the day, we'd sit with Old Crow on the ground and he'd tell us these stories about growing up in the forest. And how his relatives and friends used to eat these special berries and have wild parties and what a great long life he'd had. Judy realized, suddenly, where are they now? They've got to be around here somewhere, these relatives and friends.

That's when Old Crow told us what was coming up next for him. "As you get older," he said, "flying long distances can become difficult." Which is why he didn't go off with all the other birds this year. Sometimes the others would go off and find hot springs or caves to hang out in or they'll dig holes in the ground and cover themselves up with branches and leaves to stay warm. But not him, not this year.

Chapter 14

The Bear

The idea of Old Crow not being around any more made Judy and I feel sad. Judy asked him about going to a veterinarian if he got sick. "There has to be somebody to look after you." Old Crow laughed, actually it was more like a cackle. And just when he was about to say how ridiculous Judy's comment was, we felt the ground shake and heard branches snapping.

"If you two want to keep on living, you'd better get out of here," Old Crow said.

I turned around. About a hundred yards behind me was a bear. A big one. Black and hungry looking. Coming straight for us. "Let's go!" I yelled to Judy.

I don't know why he was coming straight at us and I didn't want to know. Maybe it was the salmon pieces that we ate. I didn't know they were his. Or maybe he just got up on the wrong side of the bed. Whatever the reason, Judy and I flew up into the closest tree and found a sturdy branch to perch on.

We looked down. Old Crow hadn't gone anywhere. He was still standing there. I shouted down at him, "Old

Crow, he's coming! Get out of there!" But Old Crow just stood his ground. He seemed to be okay with the bear running right over him. Without looking up, he said calmly, "You're going to have to go a lot higher than that." Judy and I looked at each other. What's he talking about? Bears can't climb trees.

Guess again. That bear ran right past Old Crow and started climbing up the tree we were sitting on. His claws were huge and he dug them into the tree bark as he sped higher and higher.

Judy and I flew up to the branch above us. And then the next one. And the next one. Then we flew up to the very top of the tree where there are only a couple of branches left and they are spindly and soft. We could barely balance there. The whole thing felt like it was going to tip over.

The bear was three-quarters of the way up the tree when he stopped. I couldn't believe my eyes. The guy didn't give up. He started moving his huge weight back and forth, shaking the tree. The spindly branches that we were on started to bend. I could smell the bear's breath right below us and it was terrible. Judy lost her footing. I used one of my claws to pull her back up again. Whoever said bears can't climb trees? I'd like to meet that person now, if they're still alive!

With the bear just a few feet below us, Judy and I had seen enough. We took off into the air and flew away, leaving Old Crow to do whatever he was going to do. A short while later, we circled back to find out what had happened to him. We found the exact spot where he had been standing when the bear appeared. There was nothing. No sign of him or the bear. Or anything else, for that matter. It was like they had never existed. Poof.

Sometimes I wonder about things like that. Like Old Crow and the bear who aren't around any more. Like my parents and my school and everything else that I experienced. Or thought I experienced. They all feel like dreams now. Like they'd never happened. And that everything I think happened only happened in my mind. Would that be a good thing or a bad thing? I think it would be kind of depressing. But then again, that's my mind again, right? So maybe it wouldn't be. Maybe it's like going to the movies. You buy your ticket and then you get to have an experience. Just make it a good one. Because, believe me, I've seen a lot of bad movies in my time.

Judy and I waited a while. Just to see if Old Crow would show up again. But he didn't. To get a better view, we flew up back to the branch that we'd been sitting on when the bear first attacked. It was here that I found the map. It had been stuffed into a hole in the tree where the branch was attached to the tree trunk. It was old and yellow and folded up into a flat packet like a tiny birthday present or something. On the outside, it said, "The Great Migration".

Judy and I figured it had to have been Old Crow that left it there for us. I mean, it certainly wasn't the bear. Bears don't migrate. At least none that I've heard of. And they don't use maps. But then again, I didn't know birds used maps either. I thought they all knew how to get to where they were going. Like it was baked into their genes or something. But we were birds and we didn't know where we were going. So there.

We flew the map down onto the ground and spread it out. It seemed to show exactly where we were. At least it had an 'X' on it that said: "You are here". And a squiggly route that started from "You are here" and went for hundreds of miles north into the mountains and through an area called "The Crow's Nest Pass". It then worked its way down from the mountains and onto a flat area that was called "The Great Plains".

There weren't any other lines or boundaries on the map. There was nothing regular about it except for those few words and the route itself, which had been kind of scratched onto the paper by somebody as if they hadn't been able to find a pen. Oh, there was one other thing. At the bottom of the map, it said: "DON'T BE LATE!"

Judy thought it was kind of weird that the map didn't include the city we came from or any other city or town. It just showed a series of rivers and creeks that fed into each other and formed what looked like a kind of Snakes and Ladders game that eventually led all the way across to the Great Plains, whatever they were.

We talked about what to do. Judy said that, whatever we do, we don't want to hang around there in case the bear comes back. And I said, we didn't know for sure that this was Old Crow's map and we didn't know what would be in store for us when we reached The Great Plains, if we ever did reach The Great Plains. Judy pointed out that 'having a map is better than having no map' and I said, 'but having a map that leads to death is no good either.' I don't know why I said that. It certainly wasn't helpful even though I was trying to be, and I think it just made Judy scared.

We talked about things for a while. And then we heard a strange rustling sound in the bushes beside us. That was it for me. "Let's follow the map and get the heck out of here!" I said.

I folded the map back up and tucked it into one of the two small pouches that I have hidden under my wings. As we left, I looked back and saw a tiny rabbit hip-hopping out of the bushes. I didn't tell Judy what it was because I didn't want her to know what a chicken I'd been.

Chapter 15

The Great Migration

We headed north just like it said to do on the map. Four hours later, it seemed like we'd been flying for an eternity. We stopped at a bend in the creek we were following. We drank from the creek and picked a few grubs from the nearby trees. Judy looked tired. I said that's probably good enough for one day. So, we settled in for the night. It felt like all we had was each other now. And a map that may or may not lead us to something important.

That night, as we drifted off to sleep, I counted how many nights we'd been away. I came up with four. I wondered what it was doing to our parents. If only I could have sent them some kind of signal that I was okay. But I wasn't really okay, was I? If I'd have been my parents, I should have been worried.

The police came by my parents' house again a few days after their first visit. They had some disturbing news. "Turns out, Mr Crane, the substitute teacher that was there on the day of your son's disappearance, was not a real teacher. And now nobody can find him. He's just vanished into thin air."

When Mr and Mrs Wren found out, they were furious. How could the school allow a phony teacher like Mr Crane to take over the classroom? The police officers said Mr Crane had used fake documents with a bunch of phony references about all of the schools that he'd taught at. The real substitute teacher, who was supposed to have taught that day, was Mrs Cardinal. Her file is missing from the main school board office. Not only that, but the telephone wire that led to her house had been cut the night before, so she never got the phone call to come into work. How weird is that?

My dad wasn't buying any of it. "So, you think some guy faked his way into the classroom and targeted our two kids? He spent several days teaching the students, going into the lunchroom, meeting with all the other teachers, and even hanging around after school while Judy and Roy had their detention."

My mother was beside herself. "Who is this man? Why would he do that? Why can't you find him?" Mrs Wren was equally freaked out.

"I'm with Donna. I can't believe anyone would do that."

Mr Wren shook his head. "I think it's a red herring. The guy didn't have a car. Nobody saw him drive to work. He must have come on the bus. You can't kidnap two teenagers by asking them to get on a bus." The police said they had interviewed the bus driver and everyone else who had been on the bus and nobody matching Mr Crane's description took the bus to work that morning. Nobody saw him on a bike or in a car. And none of the taxi companies had given him a ride. So, he must have walked. From where, and then to where, nobody knows. They're completely baffled.

As usual, my dad came up with the answer. "It's the Russians," he said. "It's just the kind of thing they would do. Or the Chinese. Or the Albanians." My mother's face turned red. She apologized to the police. They said it was okay. They understood. It's natural to blame others at a time like this.

"He just wants to find his son. And so do we. As soon as we find something, anything, we'll let everyone know."

After the police left, Mr and Mrs Wren opened up a cardboard box that they had brought with them. Inside, were five hundred eight-inch by ten-inch missing person posters of Judy and me, using our school annual photos. My mother was totally embarrassed.

"Oh, my god, that is such a bad photo of Roy. Seriously. I have much better ones upstairs. I'll go get them." She started for the stairs. My dad told her to not bother. He said this isn't a beauty contest. Mr Wren agreed.

"The sooner we get these up, the sooner the entire community will be out looking for them."

My dad called Spencer and Ryan in from the kitchen. "These posters have to go up immediately. On every telephone pole and every community center in the city." Ryan said he'd get right to it, just as soon as he's finished his "Age of Empires" game. Spencer said he'll get to it as well, right after he meets up with his girlfriend.

Ah, brothers, they've always got your back. My dad read them the riot act, whatever that means. Five minutes later, they had their coats on and were scurrying out the front door.

*

Judy and I did our best to follow Old Crow's map. But I've got to admit, I would have felt a lot better knowing that I was going home rather than going to wherever this map was taking us. But what choice did we have? We didn't know where home was any more. And both of us figured Old Crow wouldn't steer us wrong. He seemed to have a kind heart, plus he was on his last legs. Why would a guy with a kind heart on his last legs send us flying off in the wrong direction just before he was about to pack it in? I mean, my brothers would do that, just for fun. But hey, that's them.

We traveled north for five days. We crossed over small creeks and raging rivers and a lot of lakes of different sizes. I knew that we were flying over a plateau after we had climbed up a long way and then leveled off and not come down at all. And the trees suddenly looked different. They weren't tall and green any more. They were shorter and stubbier and there were pinecones on the ground underneath them. And it wasn't as dark on the ground any more.

At night, it got a lot colder. Thank goodness, Old Crow taught us how to puff up our feathers to keep the heat in. Otherwise, for sure, we would have become little bird-cicles.

He'd also taught us one other thing and that was to keep our feathers clean, especially the areas under our feathers where dirt and grease build up. Judy and I would splash around in some lake water or at the edge of a creek to get the dirt off. That way, it was easier for the air to get under our feathers when we puffed ourselves up.

The Crow's Nest Pass was this place where the mountains came down into a V-shape and you could travel closer to the ground between them. It went on for a couple of hundred miles and it took us several days to get through it. We knew it was the Crow's Nest because we saw a bunch of homemade signs on trees and rocks below that said things like: "Crow's Nest Pass" and "You're on The Right Track" and "Keep Up The Good Work!" They had been scratched onto the bark on tall trees and even into the dirt in open areas. Whoever made those signs, I'll never know, but it sure came in handy when we began to doubt that we were on the right track.

Chapter 16

The Premonition

Most of the time, Judy and I were in good spirits. We'd crack jokes about our classmates and make fun of the teachers that we both had. I told her that I felt bad that I hadn't ever come over to her house and that I didn't even know where she lived. She said she knew where I lived because she'd followed me home one day, or at least come part of the way home and saw which house I was in.

I asked her why she did that and she said she didn't know. "I guess I just wanted to know where you lived," she said. But I think it was more than that. I think she kind of liked me but was too afraid to say anything. But I wasn't going to say that to her because I didn't want her to feel embarrassed. And who's to say I didn't think about doing the same thing lots of times? Because, just between you and me, and let's keep it that way for now, I did. I'd always wanted to see what kind of house it was and where she ate her dinner and what her bedroom looked like. Did she have posters on the walls of Taylor Swift and Beyonce or pictures of Mario Mario and his brother, Luigi? I had no idea.

I wasn't particularly interested in what her parents looked like. I'm sure they probably looked a lot like mine. Or her brothers or sisters, if she had any. I mean, who cares about that? But what she thought about interested me, especially after I'd found out she had followed me part of the way home one day. I mean, that's big. That's got to mean something.

One night, though, I had this really bad dream. Judy and I had fallen asleep. We were perched on a pine tree, facing in opposite directions, supposedly to keep an eye out for cougars or bears or whatever else might sneak up on us. It's hard to keep one eye open when you're asleep, but I also think, as birds, we were kind of built to do that. At least I felt like I was. It was like most of my brain was asleep, but there was this tiny part of it that was still awake and looking out through my eye just in case. Whatever it was, I didn't question it because it allowed us to stay safe.

But getting back to my dream, and here was the strange part, I started having these images of a gigantic field as far as the eye can see, completely filled with birds. Millions and millions and millions of them. And I was swooping down over the top of them and making my way toward what looked like a stage, you know, like what rock bands play on. And on the stage, there was this really scary-looking bird with jet-black eyes and a snow-white face flapping his wings and shouting at all of the birds about who-knows-what; I couldn't hear what he was saying. But they seemed to be taking it all in and in total agreement with him. They'd shriek and caw and flap their wings excitedly whenever he said something.

And ever weirder, behind him on the stage, I swear, was another bird that looked just like Mr Crane. He was tall and gawky and he seemed to be keeping an eye on the crowd, just like he used to keep an eye on us when he was a substitute teacher. And then the worst thing happened. Somehow, he spotted me flying overhead. He let out a horrifying shriek and everyone looked up. Millions of bird eyeballs stared up at me. And then they all started to shriek too, like I wasn't supposed to be there or that they wanted me dead or something.

I turned around and tried to fly out of there, but for some reason, my wings felt heavy like they were coated in hot black tar or something and I started to fall. I was spinning around in circles, out of control, and I could see all of the birds below me looking up and screaming and snapping their beaks together in unison, like they were going to try and eat me. I couldn't stop. Down I went, lower and lower. And then, just as the first bird jumped up to take a bite out of me…

…I woke up. I must have let out a gasp because Judy was staring at me with a worried look. "Are you okay?" she said. I had to catch my breath. I was wild-eyed. The feathers on top of my head were sticking up. I tried to catch my breath.

"Yeah, man, wow!" Judy asked me what was going on. I told her about my dream. She felt sorry for me. Maybe it was something I ate, she said. Although, when we thought about it, we'd both been eating exactly the same stuff before we went to sleep.

Judy said she'd read all kinds of things about what happens to you when you dream. It's like the mind has a chance to think about all the crazy things it wasn't allowed to think about when you were awake.

"Why would it do that?" I asked. Judy said that it was actually a good thing because, a lot of the things we are secretly afraid of, get to play out in our dreams, as if it was a movie or TV show. Then when we see the ending and how ridiculous it all was, we're not afraid any more. She said, if it can play out in your dreams, then it doesn't have to play out in your real life. Or so the theory goes.

"I'm not sure about that," I said. "It seemed pretty real to me. And it felt like I was a goner at the end, so how am I not supposed to be afraid any more?" Judy shrugged. She didn't know. It was just some stuff that she'd read.

Even though I wasn't convinced of her theory, I thanked her for trying to figure it out. I just hoped I wouldn't have that dream any more because it was really scary. She suggested we go find some water and then get something to eat. Maybe if we both got busy, I wouldn't think so much about my dreams. After all, they're just thoughts, right?

Judy was right. But I couldn't help but think that there was something more to it. Like I'd seen into the future when maybe I wasn't supposed to. There's a word for that but I don't know what it is. Oh, yeah. Wait a minute. Premonition. Maybe I'd had a premonition.

But as far as premonitions go, you have to admit, it was a pretty lame one. What kind of a future would have millions and millions of birds jumping up and down and snapping their beaks at a no-name loser like me? I mean, what would be the point of that?

Judy and I spent the next couple of hours looking for food. And then, as soon as we felt like we'd had enough, we took off.

Chapter 17

Safe For Now

One thing about flying long distance is you get plenty of time to think about your life. In my case, I thought a lot about my parents. I wondered if they had given up. My brothers were probably figuring out who gets what of my stuff. Not that I had anything interesting. But there was my Etch-A-Sketch and a guitar that I hadn't played very much. And my comic book collection. I had tons of classic comics, like Superman and Batman, all the way back to this Donald Duck comic book from the 1950s that my grandfather gave me. I don't know if it was worth anything, but if I didn't make it home, they could have it.

After I disappeared, my parents didn't care whether my two brothers came to the table for dinner or not. The two of them just ate by themselves, mostly in silence, thinking about what they might have done to cause me to run away, that is, if I had run away. One evening at dinner, when things had gotten really quiet, there was a bang at the front door. My dad went to see what had happened. On the wicker doormat outside, there was a piece of dirty crumpled paper with a bunch of scratch marks on it. My dad turned it over, and then, upside down, and then, he was finally able to read it. It said: "Your children are safe for now."

My dad ran frantically out into the street. He looked up and down the block. There was nothing. Just some bird flying in the distance. He ran back inside and showed it to my mom.

She just about had a heart attack. "It's them! It's the kidnappers!" She insisted on phoning the police right away. And then phoning Mr and Mrs Wren. "This is good news," she exclaimed to Mrs Wren. "At least we know they're alive."

My brother, Ryan, came out of his room when he heard all of the commotion. He looked at the note, turning it over and back again, and then shrugged. "What kind of a ransom note is this? It doesn't say how much money they want. Or what they'll do to him if they don't get it. It doesn't say anything at all."

He questioned the fact that the note had been written on crumpled-up newspaper. If you want something to be read, type it out. Or at least use clean paper. My father did think that was kind of odd. Ryan pointed out that it wasn't just any old newspaper either, it was the comics. Who writes a ransom note on the comics? Maybe it's the Joker or something. My mother didn't think that was funny. I thought it was funny, but I wasn't there, so it doesn't count.

When the police finally did come, they put the note in a clear plastic bag so it could be checked for evidence. My dad added something else to a different evidence bag. A feather. He found it on the ground next to the note. It was a blue/black feather, just like the kind that the Bluebird of Happiness wore.

The police were reluctant to take it. They didn't think it had anything to do with anything. But it did, of course. A lot more than any of them knew!

At the top of Crow's Nest Pass was a place called The Pinnacle. At least that's what the map called it. It was definitely the highest point in the mountains. When Judy and I perched on the highest branch of the highest tree at the very top of the mountain, it felt like we could see forever.

We were huffing a lot. The whole way up we had been breathing heavily. Plus, the higher we went, the less energy we seemed to have. Who'd have guessed that birds can run out of oxygen just like everybody else? We stood at The Pinnacle for a few minutes, just long enough to feel proud of what we'd done, and then we started back down the other side.

We were now on the descent, halfway through the Crow's Nest Pass, and on our way toward The Great Plains. You'd think going down would be easier, but for birds, it really didn't make that much difference. We'd glide as much as possible, catching whatever rising warm air pockets there were that high up. But we still had to flap our wings most of the time.

I remember trying to add up how many flaps I'd made on the trip so far. I figured that I was probably flapping about once every two seconds on average. And we were flying about five hours a day. And we'd been gone now for what, eight days? I didn't have my calculator with me but I guessed that I'd flapped my wings about fifty thousand times since we'd left. That's a lot of flapping. If it had been my regular skinny human arms, they would have fallen off by now.

"Hurray for wings," I shouted. Judy heard me say this and wondered what I was yelling about. I was smiling. "Think what our lives would be like without these things," I said motioning to my wings. Judy smiled back. She wasn't sure what I was going on about but she could see that I was happy. Which made her happy. I realized then that that's what having another person in your life can do for you. You can make each other happy. So, instead of it being just you trying to make yourself happy all the time, there're two of you doing it, so it takes half the effort. At least that's my calculation. But then again, if you have to make the other person happy as well as yourself, doesn't that take twice the effort? I couldn't figure it out. All I knew was that she made me happy and I seemed to make her happy. And that I was no good at math. But I already knew that.

Chapter 18

A Snipe and Two Woodpeckers

It had been a long time since we'd seen Rio, or Old Crow, or any other bird for that matter. We were beginning to feel like the last two birds on the planet. When all of a sudden, we saw three beat-up-looking birds on a tree top, flapping their wings at each other and sounding like they were having an argument.

One of the birds was tiny, with a long sharp beak and spindly legs and brown/green feathers that did a great job of camouflaging him against the rest of the trees. Turned out his name was Tewksbury and he was a snipe that had come all the way from the Pacific Ocean.

The other two were woodpeckers. Their names were Barry and Chip. They lived nearby, about twenty minutes flying time away. Turns out the only reason they knew Tewksbury was because they had stumbled across him while they were flying overhead and he looked kind of skinny and didn't seem to know how to catch any bugs underneath the tree bark and so they worried that he might starve to death.

Tewksbury took issue with that. "I wasn't going to starve to death," he said. "I'm just very particular about what I eat, and for good reason. Where I come from the ocean supplies all of my culinary needs. And believe me, it offers a much better selection than what you have going on around here."

Judy and I listened to them go on and on for what seemed like forever, and we were just about to leave when Barry called out, "Enough! Look at us being rude to our new guests." Chip agreed. "Just because Tewksbury here is a food snob doesn't mean we can't be civil," he said. Tewksbury sneered at him. Then turned to us with a toothless smile. "Quite right. Why don't you thrill us with your story. Who are you and how did you end up in this fabulous part of the world?"

He was being sarcastic, of course. He didn't like the forest or the mountains at all. Judy and I figured out later on that the forest must have made him feel claustrophobic since he'd spent all of his life running around on the beaches and wide-open spaces near the ocean. I was more interested in how he ended up here, but since he asked us first, I told him. And when I mentioned the part about how we were human and got turned into birds, all three of them became instantly excited.

"How fascinating!" Tewksbury exclaimed. "Why it's like something out of the classics!" I didn't know what he was talking about. And when he started talking about some guy named Odysseus and his search for the Golden Fleece, I still didn't know what he was talking about. Turns out

Tewksbury grew up on the books that sunbathers would bring to the beach. When they went swimming in the water, or headed out for long walks along the beach, he would hop up onto their sun chairs or little side tables and flip through the pages they were reading. I wondered how he had learned to read in the first place but that seemed like another story, and frankly, our story was taking so long to finish that I was getting exhausted.

Barry and Chip were as excited as Tewksbury. They said they were honored to be in the presence of celebrities. Judy said we're not celebrities, we're just birds, no better or worse than them.

"And now that we've told you our story," she said, "how did the three of you end up here?"

Barry and Chip looked at each other. "We didn't end up here," Barry said. "This is our turf."

Chip motioned with his wings. "Fifteen minutes on both sides of this mountain is what we call home," Chip said. "Our signatures are everywhere."

What Chip was talking about were the holes they'd leave in the trees after they had finished looking for bugs. He called them signatures to make them sound important, but let's face it, they were just holes. Chip said they were just about to start The Great Migration when they stumbled across old Tewksbury here, having a hard time.

Tewksbury was about to object again, when I cut him off. "Did you say 'migration'? What migration?"

Tewksbury's beak dropped. "Uh, hello? Earth to space invaders!"

Chip and Barry burst into laughter. "What migration! Don't you get the news?"

The three of them laughed and laughed. Don't you hate it when somebody is laughing and won't tell you what's so funny? Judy and I had no idea what they were laughing about. And then, suddenly, we remembered the writing on the map that Old Crow had left us. I used my beak to pull it out of the small pocket underneath my wing and spread it out in front of us. Sure enough, at the bottom, it read: "The Great Migration".

We looked over at the others while showing them the map. "Is this what you're talking about?" Tewksbury wiped tears of laughter from his face. He leaned forward and read the bottom of the map. "I should think so," he said. He gave Barry and Chip a raised eyebrow and they broke into laughter again.

I could tell Judy was embarrassed. Obviously, this was something we should have known about but didn't. It reminded me of a lot of times at school when people would share a joke with everyone but me and it made me feel left out.

And I just didn't feel like pretending it was okay any more, so I said, "How about you three quit laughing and just tell us what's going on?"

Boy, did that put a stop to things. Chip and Barry stopped laughing immediately. I could tell they felt bad. "Of course," Barry said. "Tewksbury, why don't you explain it to them with that fancy accent of yours."

Tewksbury cleared his throat. "I'm surprised you don't know this, but most birds migrate." I said I did know that. But what's that got to do with this? "Well," he said, "this year's migration is much more important than all of the other years. The message is that all birds must migrate this year, not just some of them. And we must all migrate to a special place that has been chosen so that we can have a meeting."

Judy asked, what kind of meeting? And who sent out the message? And since when did all of the birds in the world start listening to one person, or one bird, or whatever? Barry and Chip answered each of Judy's questions in the same way.

"We don't know. We don't know. And wait a minute, we don't know."

Tewksbury pointed out that there has always been a way for birds to communicate with one another. "We've been around a long time," he reminded us, "All the way to before even the dinosaurs. And we've developed a rather ingenious method of communicating, through the air, of course. Can you imagine; out in the wild, one bird can hear another bird for up to several miles. So, it was easy to develop a relay system where a top-secret message could be sent a long way in a short period of time."

That last part sent a chill up my spine. "A top secret message? About what? And from whom?" Again, more questions and no answers. Were they keeping some kind of a top-secret message from us right now? And why would they do that since we were also birds? Nothing was making any sense. At least to me.

Barry suggested that we not get too worried about things. "We've migrated lots of times before. Like when it gets really cold out or when we get a warning message that there's a forest fire. It's just what birds do." Chip insisted that this migration wasn't anything special. It's just that everyone is supposed to do it. And that we would all be going to one place.

Judy and I had a hundred more questions to ask, but we decided that we'd hit our limit for the day and we'd better just go along with whatever Tewksbury and the two woodpeckers had planned. They certainly had more experience than us migrating. And even though they seemed like an odd trio, after a while, I kind of grew to like them.

That night, Barry and Chip made a stew out of some tasty bugs and caterpillars that they found in a tree. It was cold and mushy and horrible-looking but we were so hungry that we ate it without hesitation. Tewksbury seemed to think it was okay as well.

"Perhaps my standards are slipping," he said. "But there are flavors in here that I cannot deny have a certain appeal."

Tewksbury reminded me of myself. He was trying to pass on a compliment but somehow it sounded like an insult.

When I suggested that he just come out and say that he liked it, he said, "You must be mad! I would never go that far!"

After dinner, we sat around on tree branches talking about growing up and all of the different experiences that we'd had over the years. I told them that I'd always liked music and they said that fit.

"Fit what?" I asked.

"Well," Chip pointed out, "You're a Thrasher, are you not? And it's well known that Thrashers know up to a thousand songs." I said there's no way I know a thousand songs. I mean, I may have had a thousand songs on my cellphone back home, but I didn't know them well enough to sing them.

Judy disagreed. "I've heard you singing to yourself at school lots of times and you seem to know the words to plenty of songs."

Two things went through my brain at that point. Number one: what was she doing listening to me singing to myself at school? And number two: did I really know the words and music to all those songs? I had to find out. I told everybody to hang tough for a minute. I'm just going to try something out and it could be kind of embarrassing. Everyone went quiet.

They were all staring at me. I opened my beak slowly and began to sing. Well, tweet actually. First, one song. Then, another. Then, another. Judy was smiling. Yikes, maybe I did know a thousand songs! I went through a bunch more. Tewksbury was excited.

"Keep going," he said. "I've counted fourteen so far."

I let loose with a few more. Some of them required my voice to hit high notes that I'd never sung before. And even the low notes took me by surprise. I had a range I didn't even know existed. I looked over and the woodpeckers were swaying back and forth on their branch. It was like we were in a nightclub and I was the entertainer and I had them in the palm of my hand. Or wing. Whatever.

Over the next few minutes, I must have tweeted out a hundred different songs. And then, all of a sudden, I stopped. Judy was smiling at me. She knew all along that I had those songs in me. Maybe the others did too. But I sure didn't.

After I'd finished, Tewksbury decided that he'd have a go at a few songs himself. He tweeted out a love song, I think he called it "Sea of Love", but it was so old and lame and he was so out of tune that nobody could stand it. Barry and Chip put their wings over their ears.

Judy figured out a way to get him to stop singing without insulting him. She said, "Wait a minute, Mr Tewksbury, that song is so good, maybe we shouldn't hear it all at once. Why don't we save the rest for later." We all agreed. Tewksbury had a confused look on his face. I was amazed at how skillful Judy was. If I was as skillful as her, I bet I wouldn't have lost all those jobs that I lost a long time ago.

After that, during our evening get-togethers, Chip and Barry would always ask me to sing a song, something that I'd never sung before, and I did. I didn't know the names of most of the songs but it didn't matter. They liked what I sang and it seemed to make them feel comfortable. It's not easy being a bird, especially during the winter months, and anything that takes your mind away from your troubles, or just calms you down, is a welcome thing.

When Judy and I would go to sleep, I'd often think about my parents and how they used to complain about me listening to songs all the time on my devices. I must have had every music-playing device that was ever invented, and a pair of headphones to go with them. Plus, I had just started to learn how to play the guitar when this whole bird thing happened. I could have become a big star, but then I'd have to change my name to Conway Twitty or something what with all the tweeting. Wasn't there some famous jazz guy named 'Bird'? I could have been him.

Chapter 20

A Strange Phenomenon

Back home, my parents and brothers started to notice that strange things were happening. Birds had been vanishing. It was subtle at first. Small-town newspapers were publishing articles like 'Where O Where Have The Swallows Gone?". That one appeared in the Capistrano Gazette. And "Eagles, What Eagles?" which appeared a few days later in the Brackendale Bugle. But then the story just seemed to get bigger and bigger and started showing up on the evening news, which almost everybody watched.

My dad noticed it first. He was eating a Hungry Man dinner in front of the TV while my mother was away working at the church thrift shop, like she always does on Mondays.

My brother, Spencer, was in the kitchen with his headphones on, when my dad said, "Hey, Spence! Take a look at this." Spencer couldn't hear him, of course and had wandered back into his bedroom before my dad could get him to watch the report.

My dad recorded the news and showed it to my mother when she got home. Every year on the marshland, near where we live, the local bird watchers do a one-day bird count to see how many kinds of birds stay in the area over the winter. They usually count between twenty and thirty different species. This year, do you know how species they counted? None. And do you know why? Because not a single bird was spotted on the entire marshland.

Now my parents are no wizards when it comes to statistical analysis, or whatever you call it, but they knew enough to know that something was wrong. And since it had to do with birds, and that weird bird selfie on my cellphone was the only bit of evidence they had as to what had happened to me, they called the police officer who was in charge of the missing person's case (that's me, in case you've forgotten) and told them their theory.

They started off by saying that they thought it was quite a coincidence that birds had started to vanish and that me and Judy had vanished at almost the same time, and that there was a bird selfie on my cellphone camera. The police officer, his name was Sergeant Lark, didn't get the connection. He said it was too far-fetched to think that birds had kidnapped two children and taken them away. There was no evidence of foul play (I know, it's a bad pun, especially at this delicate time). And then he made the mistake of asking my parents if they had been drinking.

Now, my dad almost never drinks. And my mother hasn't had a drink since before I was born. So, this officer accusing my parents of being drunk or something didn't sit well with them. They had a big argument with the officer and my dad threatened to go to the newspapers if the officer didn't 'pull up his bootstraps' and start a real investigation.

The minute my dad hung up, there was another phone call. It was Mr Wren, asking if my parents had watched the evening news. They said they had. Then Mrs Wren came on the line. She said exactly what my parents had said, that it's too much of a coincidence that the children (again, that's us) disappeared just as there was a worldwide bird disappearance. There has to be a connection. My dad said that the police didn't think so. And they're not willing to act as if there is.

"The only way we're going to find Roy and Judy is if we do it ourselves."

My dad wanted to know if there had been any response to all the posters that had been put up around town. They had the Wren family's telephone number on them. Mr Wren said they received one phone call, from some crackpot named Phineas Buttonquail, who said the kids are safe and could the Wren's please send over ten pounds of birdseed to 8279 Cisticola Avenue. Mr Wren went over there with the birdseed but it turned out to be a used car lot. He hung around for an hour but nobody showed up.

I felt bad for my parents and Mr and Mrs Wren. They had no idea that we weren't kidnapped or had even run away. Judy and I weren't prisoners. We were free. We could have gone anywhere at any time. Nobody was forcing us to do anything.

My dad was close though when he said we might have been kidnapped by birds. I mean, birds were involved, for sure. But it's like they say, or at least somebody said, close only matters in horseshoes and hand grenades. And since nobody we knew had any of those particular items, or even knew where to find them, my dad's theory was rejected.

Travelling with Tewksbury and the woodpeckers felt natural after a while. Neither Judy nor I had made many friends in our lives. I told you about Leonard and the Thrashers and how all that turned out. So, heading through the mountains with those three guys felt good.

Tewksbury taught us a game that we could all play. He read it in a book of games that he came across on the beach. It was a kind of bingo, only we used these dried-up berries with numbers scratched on them as the bingo balls. And instead of yelling out 'Bingo!' when you'd filled in all of the numbers, you had to yell out "Tewksbury", which, of course, was his name. He said it was only fitting since he came up with the game. I pointed out that the game would have gone a lot quicker if we used the name "Roy" or "Judy", but he didn't care. It was his game and people didn't have to play it if they didn't want to.

We played it though, every night, because we'd run out of things to talk about and it was fun. I'd watched my parents play bingo before. Usually, there was a prize that you could win like a lamp or an ashtray. The other birds didn't know what those things were so we settled on prizes like 'two dead bugs' or 'one fat worm' or 'a bunch of squished ants'. I know that doesn't sound like much, but what were we going to do with a lamp or an ashtray? None of us even smoked.

Between playing bird bingo and singing songs, and watching the moon rise and staring up at the stars, I think all of us became friends. And soon, all the differences between us felt like good things instead of problems. I mean, can you imagine what life would be like if everybody was exactly the same size or talked the same way and had the same thoughts? In the bird world, there must be thousands of different kinds of birds and none of them are the same. It wasn't long before Judy and I discovered first-hand just how many birds there are in the world. But as usual, I'm getting ahead of myself.

Chapter 21

Migration Nation

As the Crow's Nest Pass headed down out of the mountains and out into the foothills, we began to see more and more birds who looked like us. They were tired and kind of beat-up-looking with missing feathers. And whatever formation they were flying in at the beginning of their trip, had deteriorated to the point where they were just barely able to fly alongside each other, trying to keep up.

There was owls and chickadees and thrushes and warblers and crows and goldfinches and cockatoos. Most of them were in groups of the same species, but some of the flocks had mixed together, probably like what had happened to Tewksbury and the woodpeckers and us; thrown together by circumstance and thinking to themselves, 'Hey? What's wrong with making new friends?'

Just as we came down off the foothills, something major happened. A huge line of birds that had been traveling north from down south, ran right into our group who had been travelling east from out of the mountains. Some of the southerners were parrots that looked like flying paintings with streaks of green and red and orange feathers and bulging eyes. One of the birds shouted at us, "Where are you going? Head north! Head north!"

Judy and I didn't know what to do. I started to reach for the map that Old Crow had given us when I noticed that Barry and Chip had already started to join them and Tewksbury was motioning for us to do the same.

"You have to head north," he said, "otherwise you'll get left behind." I was about to ask, 'Why north?" but Tewksbury was already gone.

Before we knew it, Judy and I were a part of something that was truly unbelievable. Thousands and thousands of birds had joined into one long line that stretched for miles. I tried to see how far it went back behind us, but I couldn't. And if any of us slowed down or sped up or tried even the slightest to see what was going on around us, we'd get bumped by the bird that was flying behind us, or wind up with our nose pointed into the rear end of the bird that was flying in front of us.

Now, I've never had much to do with the military but this sure felt like we were marching. Not on the ground, but in the air, with loose feathers floating around everywhere. And then there would be this great 'whooshing' sound, as sometimes our wings would beat at the same time.

Wherever we were going, it was exciting. Maybe it was the feeling of belonging to something bigger than us, but I know that we both felt it. Judy's face was flush. And I seemed to have unlimited energy. Plus, there's this thing about flying in a group, where those in front of you are deflecting the wind so that you don't have to fly quite as hard. If you've ever been in a car on the highway and you pull in behind a big truck, my dad says it's like you're hardly driving at all.

There were birds flying above us and below. I had this thought. I wondered how many of them used to be human. Was it just Judy and me or were there others as well? And what about Rio and Old Crow? Were they still alive and were they a part of this too?

Mile after mile we kept going. And then something happened that worried me. Sometime in the late afternoon, Judy angled downward, flying lower and lower in the flock. I followed her down, of course, just to see what was going on. She said she was feeling hungry and was running out of energy. I said, 'Okay, let's land somewhere and get something to eat."

The birds around us couldn't figure out what we were doing. They all gave us looks like we were crazy as we descended toward the rolling foothills and scrubby pine trees below.

Judy and I landed on a hill next to a tiny lake. We looked up. Overhead, the sky was black with birds, thousands and thousands of them, and they weren't stopping for anything, I could tell.

After a few minutes, the flock seemed to end and we could see the sky again. It got really quiet. I looked over at Judy. She was scratching at the ground and pulling up bugs and worms already. It felt kind of weird not being with the flock. And part of me wanted Judy to hurry up so we could re-join them.

And then Judy said something that made me start to doubt things. She said, "Don't you think it's weird that we're going north?" I didn't know what she was talking about. And then she said, "I always thought birds went south for the winter."

I hadn't thought about it. I know there were a couple of times that my parents drove south down to Mexico with us kids but that was during summer vacation, and it made sense because we were all out of school and were driving my parents crazy at home anyway.

"No," Judy said, "I'm almost positive. Birds fly south in the winter and come back up north in the spring and summer." And then I shrugged and said something stupid again, like I often do at times, like this, "Well, these ones don't."

Judy shook her head and kept digging for worms. She tossed a few juicy ones into the air and swallowed them. I stumbled across a few beetles myself and ate those. I wasn't as hungry as Judy, and pretty soon, I was saying things like, "Welp, that's it for me," and "You almost done?" I think Judy was happy just to have a few quiet moments to herself and she probably didn't need some doofus like me telling her to keep moving.

But there was something about not being with the flock that made me uncomfortable. Judy didn't feel it as strongly as me. She said, "What if we stayed here for a couple of days? This is nice." I didn't think it was a good idea and I told her.

"What makes you say that?" she asked. I didn't know. I just felt kind of weird not being with the group. She said, "Okay, tell you what, we'll go over that hill over there and see what's on the other side, and if we don't like what we see, we'll re-join the group." That seemed fair enough, so I said, sure.

Instead of flying over the hill, for some reason, we decided to take a walk. It was a nice afternoon. Perfect for a stroll. And from my perspective, who better to have a nice stroll with than Judy?

As we neared the crest of the hill, I could hear a faint buzzing sound, like a hive of bees, coming from the other side. Judy was puzzled. I got kind of worried. I hadn't thought about bees and I didn't know whether they would sting birds or not. I only know that I'd been stung at summer camp one year, and I remember it to this day for a reason.

As we crested the hill, I could see that it wasn't bees. It was birds. Thousands of them. And they were being very quiet. Just standing in groups as if waiting for something.

From out of the flock, near the front, waddled Tewksbury and the two woodpeckers, Barry and Chip. "Hey," Barry said. "How's it going?"

Chip added, "We were worried about you." I looked around. "You mean everybody?"

Tewksbury grinned. "Of course, my good friend. All of us. We thought something might have happened to you."

Judy was embarrassed. She had no idea that everyone was concerned about us. "I got hungry, so we stopped for food," she said timidly.

Tewksbury smiled. "Don't feel bad. That was an excellent idea! As you can see, a lot of us were thinking the very same thing." He turned around. A lot of the birds were now pecking at the ground as if searching for food.

"You see, Judy?" I said, "They're only thinking of us." Judy struggled to get over her embarrassment.

She said, "I'm sorry. I didn't know you were waiting for us, otherwise, I would have kept going."

"Nonsense," Tewksbury said, "Take as long as you'd like. In the great scheme of things, after a million years of evolution, what's a few more minutes?"

Barry and Chip laughed. I thought it was funny too. Birds have been around for a long time, well, you get the idea. Anyway, Judy said she was finished and that we should probably get going.

Tewksbury agreed. "Between now and sunset, I'll bet we can squeeze in another hundred miles!"

The instant Judy and I took off from the hill, all of the birds took flight at once. Have you ever seen that happen? A huge flock of birds taking off at exactly the same time? Well, it was happening to us, and we were right in the middle of it, and it felt incredible.

Chapter 22

The Reward

Before we knew it, we were back in formation. A long line of birds probably five hundred feet thick, flying in the same direction at the same speed. No air force in the world could have done what we were doing. And Judy and I had hardly any training either. It seemed to come naturally to us, sort of like it was built in. Like Tewksbury said, "After a million years of evolution…" Well, you get the idea.

The further north we went, the colder it got. I kept thinking about my family. Had they forgotten about me already? Had they put my kitchen chair off to the side and rented out my room to some other kid?

As it turns out, my dad and Mr Wren had decided to offer a reward to anyone who had information about what happened to us. Mr Wren didn't have much money, so my dad suggested he put up two hundred and fifty dollars and my dad would put up seven hundred and fifty, and that way, they could offer a grand total of a thousand dollars and it would seem like a lot. They printed up some new posters with better pictures on them, along with the reward money.

Man, a thousand dollars. If I'd known that, I would have turned myself in and collected the money myself. Imagine what I could have bought with a thousand dollars. My dad probably wouldn't have been very happy about it, but maybe he would have been so glad to see me that he would have let it go. What do you think?

The posters did bring in some information, but none of it was any good. Some lady, who signed her name, 'Mrs X', said she had actual evidence that we'd been taken to Jupiter by these mysterious lizard people. She sent my parents a photo, which was obviously a fake, of a picture of Jupiter with two lizards on it that were guarding a cage that had Judy and me inside of it. Needless to say, she didn't get any of the money. I mean, the lizard thing was believable, but on Jupiter? Get real!

One night, my mom and dad were sitting in the living room watching an old episode of this show called, "Gunsmoke", when something hit the living room window with a WHAM! It freaked them both out. There were feathers and some other stuff all mushed up against the glass.

My dad went outside and looked around. He found a bird with grey/blue feathers staggering around in the bushes. It came to its senses a couple of minutes later and flew off. My dad was happy that the bird was okay. But he didn't check the bushes where the bird had landed. If he had, he would have seen a crumpled-up note that said, "May the bluebird of happiness grant your wishes!"

He went inside and told my mother that it was a bird that hit the window and that it was okay. My mom was happy, but she would have been a whole lot happier if they had found the note and put two and two together and figured out that Judy and I had stumbled across that very same bird and made a wish that was coming true right now.

But they didn't. And the note stayed buried in the bushes. And that bird, which was one of the last to be seen in the area, took off north and blended in with all the other birds and never wrote any more notes. And I know that sounds depressing but it's true. Well, not entirely true, as you'll see. What's the title of that James Bond movie, "Never Say Never Again"? Well, that's like this. Only there's no James Bond character and no guns or car chases or anything. But there's other stuff that I think is a lot more exciting, as you'll see.

Oh, one last thing about Judy's and my parents. The police searched all over the school grounds for clues as to where we had gone, and they found this brown hairclip under the back stairs where Judy and I first met after becoming birds. They showed it to Judy's mom. She confirmed that it was probably Judy's only she couldn't be sure. Judy had other brown clips just like it, but lots of kids had them.

The police said there was no way that anyone could have dropped that clip in the place where they found it. The space under the stairs was so small that only a cat or a bird could have made its way in there. Mrs Wren started to worry. She couldn't figure out what the police were saying.

She just wanted to know where her daughter was and so did Mr Wren.

Telling somebody that their daughter's hairclip was found in some place that was impossible to get to is probably not the best thing to say to two worried parents. It freaks me out just telling you about it, and I know how it got there and everything there is to know. Well, almost.

Chapter 23

Arrival

I counted. We'd been gone fifteen days and fifteen nights. The mountains had turned into foothills and then into these low grassy plains that seemed to go on forever. I didn't know where we were but it was cold.

Huge flocks of birds had been coming in wide streams and joining us from every direction. Some of them must have come from Europe and Africa, at least they looked pretty exotic with their colorful feathers and weird beaks and everything. But I think everybody looks weird to everybody else when you first meet them, so what's the difference?

At night, if the moon was bright enough, Judy and I would lie awake and secretly study the map that Old Crow had given us. As I said before, there weren't any names on it, but we could sort of figure out where we were by the shape of the land.

We thought we must be close to the Arctic Circle, maybe Baffin Island after this long stretch of water that we went over, although it was hard to say. Wherever it was, the ground looked like it had been frozen for a long time.

I guess one of the good things about being a bird is that the cold doesn't bother your feet as much.

When I was a human, if I took my runners and socks off and went into the water, even in the summertime, my feet got cold. They were always cold. Same with my hands and fingers. But as a bird, my feet were dry and scaly and I don't think there was a ton of blood flowing through there. Plus, my heart just seemed to be beating a lot faster so maybe I had better circulation. Who knows? I'm no bird doctor. And frankly, I'm not even sure those exist.

Either way, the cold didn't seem to bug Judy or me. The more colorful birds complained a lot. I heard them griping about the dampness and how they were looking forward to getting back home again. But if you were from Africa or some other hot place, you probably wouldn't think that coming to this area was any dream picnic.

By the time we'd reached day seventeen, I could tell something was happening. There were a lot of birds that seemed to be bunching up in the air and then circling around in what looked like giant clouds of birds. If you know what a galaxy looks like, and I've seen lots of them in books about astronomy, it kind of looked like that. Swirling around and then spiraling inward toward some kind of a center.

Judy and I could feel an energy in the air. The birds around us were getting excited. Maybe they were just exhausted and looking forward to a rest. But it seemed to be more than that. As though maybe we had finally reached our destination.

We must have been about a thousand feet up when this great circle of hills came into view. In the foreground, the sky was dark with birds, like some weird alien mass that had formed into a slow-moving circle.

We started to descend with the others, not wanting to drop too quickly or too slowly for fear of bumping up or down against the others, which would cause us to lose our place, our precious place within in the group.

As we circled downward, I could tell this was it. This was where we were supposed to be. A huge snowy area that went on for miles and miles, surrounded by hills that blocked the view of anyone except those who were in it. And my guess is, unless you were a bird, you probably didn't want to be here anyway.

Judy and I felt like strangers, but at the same time, we knew that we weren't. We were somehow part of this. Whether it was because of our wish and the bluebird of happiness, or Mr Crane, or Old Crow, or any of the other birds that we'd met along the way, we had no idea. We only knew how we felt. That we were part of something tremendous. Something bigger than both of us. And that we wanted to see what came next.

Chapter 24

The Seance

Back home, my parents did everything they could to keep their spirits up. On Ryan's birthday, which was the same day that us birds arrived at the circle of hills after the great migration, my mom baked a cake and they ordered in some Chinese food and tried to pretend that everything was okay. But everybody was glum.

Ryan said my parents and Spencer shouldn't pretend that everything was good because it wasn't. But no matter how sad everyone was, they still piled into that Chinese food like there was no tomorrow. And I'm glad about that. Not because I think that I'm not worth saying no to Chinese for, but I mean, why waste it? Somebody went to a lot of work to make that food. The least they could do is eat it.

At the end of the dinner, everybody opened up their fortune cookies. Now, I've eaten a lot of Chinese food and opened up a lot of fortune cookies where the fortunes were printed poorly or in French or Spanish or something, but I've never heard of four people opening up four fortune cookies all at the same dinner and finding absolutely nothing inside.

My dad got on the phone right away and called the Dragon Inn Restaurant looking for answers. The guy at the other end of the line couldn't explain it. It was the first time this had ever happened to him in over thirty years of being open for business. He apologized over and over and told my dad that he could have his money back for the entire meal if he wanted. But my dad settled down and took pity on him and said no, it was okay.

My mom was really upset. Spencer said maybe it was a good thing. At least it wasn't a bad fortune. I'd take no fortune over a bad fortune any day, but I wouldn't take no food over bad food. I'll eat bad food as long as I don't have to pay for it.

Anyway, it was right about that time that Ryan heard some cat mewing loudly outside. He got everybody to be quiet so that he could hear. Sure enough, there it was, plain as day. Spencer ran over to the front door and opened it.

Spencer looked down. Seated right in front of him on the welcome mat was a tiny black cat. And just in front of the cat was that crumpled-up note from the bushes. See? I told you 'Never Say Never Again'. Just like Mr Bond.

Spencer read the note out loud. "May the bluebird of happiness grant your wishes!" He turned to my parents who looked completely baffled. He turned back to the cat, but the cat was gone. He looked around. All he could see was Mr and Mrs Wren walking toward the house from down the block.

"Hey, Dad? I think the Wrens are here."

My parents greeted Mr and Mrs Wren and asked them what they were doing there. Mr Wren was embarrassed. Mrs Wren said, "Look, we don't seem to be getting anywhere with the police so I thought about trying something else. What about a séance?" My dad's heart sank. He looked over at Ryan and Spencer. They rolled their eyes.

"Mrs Wren, we don't believe our children are gone," my dad said. "We only know that they're missing." Mrs Wren pointed out that séances aren't just for the dead, they're for spirits that are alive too.

"I think we should be willing to try anything that might give us a clue as to where they are."

My mother thought it wasn't a bad idea. Then Spencer came up with his brilliant idea. "Look, I just found this outside on the mat. It says, 'May the bluebird of happiness grant your wishes.' Why don't we try that first?"

There was a brief discussion about which should come first, or whether they should be doing anything at all. But my mom and Mrs Wren struck a compromise. They'll perform the séance as long as they all can get together first and hold hands with each other and make a wish for the safe return of Roy and Judy.

Now, there aren't a lot of things in life where I wish I could have been there, but this was one of them. And it had nothing to do with a séance or making a wish. It had to do with the fact that I know both Ryan and Spencer hate holding hands. With anyone. They don't even like holding their own hands, let alone each other's or some stranger's from down the block.

So, when it came time for everyone to sit around the dining room table that was still littered with Chinese food boxes and hold hands... greasy, smelly, sticky hands... and wish for me, their little brother, a safe return, Spencer almost threw up. Ryan gagged a couple of times. My dad kept his eye on them and growled occasionally, but they made it through the wish. And so, that wish was registered by whoever keeps track of those things and that was the first part.

Then it came time for the séance. Have you ever seen a séance performed in the movies? Well, it was nothing like that. This one was flat, boring, uncomfortable and embarrassing. Mrs Wren did her best to appear mysterious and spiritual, but nobody believed it. Nobody heard any voices. Nothing moved.

After a while, Spencer left to be with his girlfriend and Ryan excused himself to return to his 'Age of Empires' game. By the end of the evening, my dad brought out the bourbon and he and Mr Wren were talking sports. Another day spent trying to find Roy and Judy. And another big fat zero to show for it.

But Judy and I knew exactly where we were. We were at the biggest gathering of birds that had ever taken place in the history of bird-dom, or whatever you want to call it.

Judy and I found a spot to land on a tiny piece of tundra. We looked around. Birds were everywhere. Tufts of feathers. Beaks sticking into the air. Clucking and cawing and flapping. All of it respectful, of course, but totally overwhelming.

I was trying to remember where I had seen this kind of thing before. And then I remembered a movie that I saw about Woodstock, this giant rock concert that happened way before Judy and I were born. At that concert it was the same thing, nothing but people as far as the eye can see. And noisy. And smelly. And you couldn't see what was going on half the time, but it didn't matter. Everyone was having a good time celebrating each other and how great it felt to be alive.

I looked at Judy. "Are you okay?" I asked.

She nodded. "Yes! It's very exciting!" I nodded in agreement. For some reason, I felt like I needed to take care of her, to make sure she was celebrating, like they did at Woodstock, although I wasn't really sure what we were celebrating.

But instead, I said something stupid like always. "Would you rather be here or taking a math test in Mrs Algonquin's class?" Judy gave me a confused look.

"What do you mean?" she said. I shrugged. I didn't know what I meant.

"Forget I said that." If I could have wound back the clock thirty seconds, I would have.

I gave her an embarrassed look. And then something popped into my mind which was even more regrettable. "I'm going to see if I can find Tewksbury and the others." Judy nodded. I could see she didn't want me to go. "Don't worry," I said. I'll be right back." She nodded again.

The moment I flew up and above the crowd, I knew it wasn't the right thing to do. But I kept going because I didn't want Judy to see that I was worried. I had to be careful not to hit anyone else who might be rising up.

I soared at least ten feet above the ground, just over everyone's heads. There were thousands and thousands of birds. Some were dancing together. I could hear a drum beating in the distance.

I traveled about half a mile when this giant stage came into view on the horizon. It was made out of bamboo poles that must have been flown up here by some kind of bird, along with enough rope to lash them together. On the stage was a platform made from chipped-out blocks of ice that had been covered in leaves and branches. And facing the stage, there were hundreds of reflectors made from ice that focused the sunlight down and lit everything up. It looked like some gigantic Broadway show, although, never having been to Broadway myself, I wouldn't know.

I circled high above the stage. I could see teams of birds below, setting up refreshment stands where you could get water or a bug or worm snack. There were places where you could rest in case you ran out of energy. And a giant screen made of ice where whoever was talking could put up a picture or something.

In the distance, more birds kept arriving. All the time, more and more birds. They flew over the tops of the hills, soaring down into the icy valley and filling up the empty spots that remained, although there weren't many left at this point.

As the spaces filled up, they became one solid mass of color. That's when it hit me. Which direction had I come from to get to the stage? Had I come from behind the stage or the front or off to the side? And how far had I flown after I took off? But most of all, how the heck was I going to find Judy?

Chapter 25

The Speech

From the stage below, a weird sound could be heard. It was one bird talking. But all the birds in front of him repeated the sound instantly which caused it to be amplified. Then the sound moved like a wave back through the crowd, so that everyone could hear it. It was like an echo, only one that had no delay.

"Welcome all birds!" it said. "Prepare yourself. We are about to begin." The sound whooshed through the crowd. I was about two hundred feet off the ground. Trying desperately to return to the spot where I had left Judy.

Other birds approached who looked equally lost. Some of them would zoom up and flutter right alongside me. "Have you seen this yellow-throated warbler, kind of silly looking, got this gold and purple stripe underneath?" I'd shake my head and off they'd fly.

And then another would approach. "I'm looking for my son. He's a duck."

I'd say, "There're ten million ducks down there."

And they'd say, "He has a green head and a yellow bill."

And I'd say, "Half of them have green heads and yellow bills." And then they'd give me this frustrated look and fly off.

I moved in ever-widening circles over the crowd. I was hoping that Judy had also been told by her father to stay put when she was lost. And then I realized, wait a minute, I'm the one who is lost, not her. But there's no point in me staying put because nobody's looking for me. So, I just kept going.

I flew closer to the ground. After ten minutes, I started to get tired. It's not easy flying low. There are no up draughts or currents you can catch hold of. And you always have to watch out for other birds taking off. Plus, I was looking at faces. Thousands and thousands of faces. Different colors and shapes and sizes. Tiny birds propped up on bigger birds' shoulders. Hundreds of the same species hanging out together.

Pheasants, geese, cormorants, flamingos, hummingbirds. Everyone chattering and squawking and screaming. Nobody seemed to be paying any attention to any of the instructions that were coming from the stage. "All right, everyone. Please calm down. We know you're excited. We are about to begin."

Doves, quail, eagles, storks, chickens. Chickens? How the heck did they get here? I guess any bird can get anywhere if they put their minds to it. Masses and masses of birds. And nowhere to land. A sea of feathers and beaks and eyeballs.

I was down to about ten feet off the ground now, soaring over everyone's heads, quickly losing energy, preparing to crash into the crowd. Ready for the fact they might tell me I had to leave. And that I might never see Judy again. She would have to take off with everyone else when this was over. She'd have no choice. It was either that or freeze to death.

As my tailfeathers brushed up against the tops of a few bird heads that were below me, I lowered my feet and closed my eyes, preparing for a hard landing. And then I heard a voice.

"Roy!" I opened my eyes. Twenty feet away, Judy's tiny face was poking up out of the crowd.

"Over here!" She was flapping her wings and jumping up and down.

I spun around in mid-air, doing a complete about-face, and performed a miraculous landing, jamming myself in between her and her neighbor, and then looking at her as if nothing had happened.

"Where were you?" she said, "What took you so long?" I pretended to be calm and easygoing about everything which, of course, I was anything but.

"Oh, I just wanted to look at a few things. Were you worried?"

Judy pretended not to be. "I knew you'd be back," she said. "I just didn't want you to miss out on the beginning of the event." I nodded and smiled. I think we both knew we were worried about each other. I was definitely relieved to be back standing alongside her. And it didn't bother me at all that we were squished together and that our feathers were touching. In fact, I kind of liked it.

At that point, the event began. In the distance, I could see a group of birds making their way out onto the stage. One of them was a penguin, which was really weird. And then there was this tall, lanky character that looked a lot like Mr Crane but it was hard to tell because he was so far away.

In the middle of the group, was an unusually large parrot with grey/green feathers and a short, stubby beak. But what really caught my attention was his face—it looked like a white cloud with two dark eyes sticking out of it that never seemed to blink. As he moved to the front of the stage, everyone stepped aside to make way for him. And when he looked out, it was with this stare as though he was trying to hypnotize us or something.

I asked Judy what kind of bird he was. She shook her head. "I think it's a kea, but I'm not sure." she said. "If it is, they're from New Zealand."

Now, I don't know what effect most birds have on other birds, but when this parrot talked, everybody got really quiet.

Judy leaned over and whispered to me, "Kea's are super smart!" she said.

"How smart?" I asked.

She said, "I think they're the smartest birds in the world." And then she shushed me. Which didn't feel very good. Nobody likes to be shushed.

"I am Whiteface!" the parrot bellowed. "Most of you know me already. And those of you who don't are about to!"

I remember thinking: "Duh. If you don't know somebody, and they introduce themselves to you, of course, you'll know them after that."

I don't know about you, but I've noticed that people, and birds, say the most obvious stuff sometimes, and for some reason, everybody thinks it's cool, but it's not. Anyway, I figured now was not the best time to mention it to Judy.

As Whiteface continued, off to the side, a picture appeared like magic on the giant ice monitor. It showed a small group of dinosaurs with a bunch of birds flying around overhead.

"Birds have been around for millions of years," he said. "Long before dinosaurs ruled the world." There was a lot of clucking and cooing at that comment, as if everyone agreed. "And we intend to be around for millions of years more!"

That set everyone off. They started cawing and shrieking and flapping their wings. Feathers were flying everywhere.

I looked over at Judy and even she was excited. "Yes," she said to me, "Millions of years." I remember thinking that I'm twelve years old now, so a million more years would be a pretty good deal. Tons of time for video games and watching TV. What I didn't realize, of course, was that he wasn't saying that I'd be around for millions of years. He was talking about birds in general.

Somebody offered Whiteface a drink of water and wiped his face with a cloth made out of feathers.

"Most humans think we are dinosaurs," he said, "and they wonder why we just don't go the way of the dinosaur and become extinct. Well, I have an answer to that. We are not dinosaurs! We are birds and we rule this world!"

Well, that did it. The crowd exploded with excitement. Birds were flying around, banging into each other, yelling and shrieking, and I have to say, that there was even some unexpected pooping that came along as a result.

Now, most birds don't mind pooping in front of each other. But they don't like getting pooped on. So, when some birds got angry, Whiteface tried to calm them down.

"Please, everyone. Let's get down to business."

I didn't know kind of what business we had to do, or, for that matter, what we were even doing here. But it wasn't long before I found out.

On one half of the screen next to Whiteface, was a picture of a group of humans that looked sort of like cartoons, and on the other half was a picture of a group of birds. And in the middle was what looked like a big cloud of smoke.

"For millions of years, we have been living on this planet without problems. We have lived in peace, with lots of food to eat and plenty of fresh air and water. We have woken up every morning and not had to think about anything except our families and getting food and where the closest water supply is. We knew where it was. It was always close by."

A voice from the crowd yelled, "Yes. Always close by. Here, here." It sounded like Tewksbury with his strange accent, but I couldn't be sure.

Whiteface continued, "But all that has changed. Humans have made sure of that. They've created enough smoke and hot air so that the places where food used to be plentiful aren't plentiful any more. And the water that used to be close by doesn't taste good any more. And that can't go on."

Whiteface turned around. Behind him, the bird that looked a lot like Mr Crane waddled forward and presented him with a white book. Whiteface held it up in the air.

"Most of you have read this book. It's called The Last Cycle. It is the only book that I have written. And the only book that I will ever write. And if you haven't read it yet, you should be ashamed of yourself!"

Judy and I felt ashamed. Neither of us had read it. In fact, we'd never even heard of it. Furthermore, neither of us knew that birds could read. And frankly, I'm still not sure of that.

"We'd better read it," Judy said, "or we're going to be in trouble." I agreed. What else was I going to say? It was like being the team captain in the Stanley Cup or the Superbowl and turning to the guy next to you and saying, "You know what, I've never really liked this game." It was just asking for trouble.

Whiteface opened up the book. He turned to a page that had a marker on it. "Listen, and understand," he said. "This is what humans think of their place in the world. It is taken directly from their primary source of knowledge, the Internet."

He sighed. Then started reading. "Not only have humans become the most dominant species on the planet, but they have also become, by far, its most intelligent, adaptable and resourceful species. This outcome is the result of some very fortunate events that have happened to humans along their evolutionary pathway."

The crowd booed. Only it wasn't just a regular boo like you'd hear if a comedian wasn't funny or if your team got scored against. It was more like a powerful chanting of "Boo! Boo! Boo!" that got so loud you couldn't hear anything else.

Whiteface flapped his wings to settle everyone down. "Now, I don't know about you. But where I come from, adaptable and intelligent doesn't mean you go around ruining all the drinking water and cutting down all the trees in the forest. Nor does it mean building giant houses for just one or two people that you heat all day long when you're not even there."

He had a point. I thought about my parent's place and all the times there would be nobody home and we'd keep the heat on. And the newspapers we used to get every day that had sections in it that nobody even read. I mean, what was the point of that?

Whiteface continued, "Adaptable means changing how you fit in with a changing environment, not changing the environment to fit in with you. That doesn't work. It has never worked in the past. And it's not working now."

The crowd around us agreed in unison. "That doesn't work! That doesn't work!" It was like the same mind shouting out with a million different voices.

Whiteface went on, "But that's about to change. Because dominant doesn't mean destroy. This planet has already created a species that is dominant because it is adaptable. It fits in with the environment. It migrates and moves around and uses only the energy it consumes. It changes to fit in with an ever-changing world. That dominant species is us. We are birds!"

There was a great wave of chanting "Birds. Birds. Birds".

Whiteface said that, for many years, birds have been passive. "We have been acting as if humans were dominant. They are not dominant. They are not adaptable. They are destroying the only home we have. The only home we will ever have. They are fools." The crowd erupted. "Fools. Fools. Fools."

"With this great migration," Whiteface shouted, "with this gathering of all the birds in the world, we are about to change that! And tomorrow, I will show you how!" The crowd went nuts. "Show us. Show us. Show us."

I was worried. Everybody became so agitated. I looked over at Judy but she didn't seem to be troubled at all. "Isn't this great?" she said. "He is so wonderful!" She was referring to Whiteface, of course, not me. Although I wish it was the other way around.

Whiteface turned and waddled off the stage. A light shone on one of his helpers. It was definitely Mr Crane. He was unmistakable. Super tall. Skinny. With that ultra-long beak of his and the tuft of hair sticking out of the back of his head. And those black beady little eyes. I'd know him anywhere. What was he doing here? And how did he come to be Whiteface's right-hand man? Or bird.

Chapter 26

Darker Than Dark

I was hoping that the speech Whiteface gave would answer all of my questions. But all it did was create more questions. What was the big change Whiteface was talking about? Why did he have to wait until tomorrow before telling us? And what were we supposed to do in the meantime? Just stand there?

The crowd settled in for the night. I was surprised at how small birds can get when they go to sleep. They lie on the ground or stand and curl up against each other to share their heat. Like Whiteface said, they adapt to their environment. They don't try and change it. Unlike a lot of humans that I know.

Judy and I did the same. I mean, what choice did we have? The crowd was so thick, all you had to do was drop to the ground and curl up together. We were both exhausted. The last thing I remembered was staring into her eyes as we fell asleep.

I had a weird dream that night. About all the stuff that got wasted by me over the years: all of the pop cans and food wrappers, toilet paper, the diapers and clothing that got thrown into the garbage. I mean, where did it all go? I never saw any of it, that's for sure.

I remember going to the dump once with my dad, but it was so smelly that I stayed in the car. There were old mattresses out there, and rusty bicycles, and old beat-up stoves and fridges. And plenty of birds. They'd be flying around in circles looking for any food that we'd thrown away. They were adapting to the environment. What were we doing? I don't know. Just not thinking about it.

That night, in the crowd, I also dreamt that I had invented a space suit that humans could wear all the time on earth. I called it 'The Roy Thrasher Earth Suit'. All the heat, water, and food that you ever needed would be built right in. All you had to do was walk around and be normal and happy and live your life and not waste stuff all the time. You'd poop, of course, but there would be this area in the back of the suit that collected it all and you'd dump it out at night. And the stuff that you dumped out could be used as fertilizer if you had a garden.

A lot of times things don't make sense in your dreams. But sometimes they do. And when I woke up in the middle of the night, I was so excited about my 'Roy Thrasher Earth Suit' that I thought about waking Judy up and telling her. But I didn't. And I'm glad I didn't. She would have killed me. But then again, she might have been so excited by my idea that it would have been okay. Who knows?

I had a second dream that I forgot to mention. Only it wasn't a good one. I dreamt that my parents had adopted another boy to take my place. And everyone seemed to like him a lot, although I couldn't see what he looked like because he was always turned away. He was tall and thin and kind of awkward looking.

I would see him at the kitchen table, sitting in my chair, lowering his head down to eat his food and then raising it back up again to swallow. And I had the worst feeling in my stomach that I knew this person.

And sure enough, when he turned around, my heart sank. It was Mr Crane, only younger and gawkier than when I first met him. And my mother said, "Roy, I'd like you to meet your brand-new brother." I'm pretty sure I let out a scream and that's when I woke up. I was covered in bird sweat.

I lay awake for a while, catching my breath, staring over at Judy, and listening to all the wheezing and hollow breathing sounds coming from the birds. In the cold air, steam rose from their bodies like feathery clouds.

I remember thinking 'how did I get here?' I thought about how everything had changed when Mr Crane came to the school but that it wasn't him that had actually changed things. It was that bluebird of happiness that crashed into the window. He granted us the two wishes Judy and I made. He's the one that turned us into birds so that we could come all the way up to this place. I wondered where he was now. Did he know what he'd done? Had he planned all of this? Again, more questions.

I must have fallen asleep again because, when I awoke up, I was listening to music. Not the kind of music that you probably listen to. No, this was 'bird music'. A rhythmic thumping of wings with a lot of humming and chirping and whistling. I could have been in a forest somewhere or in the Amazon. These birds were from all over the world. And every morning, they'd wake up and play the same music. So why should today be any different?

It was comforting in a way. I felt like I had become part of something that was bigger than myself, or Judy, or my parents and brothers. This was the music of the world and it had been around for probably millions of years.

Judy opened her eyes. It must have freaked her out to see that I was laying there staring at her. But she smiled anyway and yawned and pretended it was okay.

"How long have you been awake?" she asked. I said only a few minutes. But really, I'd been awake for an hour. I just liked staring at her. A lot of other birds were already awake. A few of them were flying around overhead, looking for friends or what have you.

I was just about to ask Judy what she thought was going to happen today, when the crackling voice of Mr Crane came over the 'ice speaker'. "Attention everyone. Whiteface will be arriving shortly," he said. "Stand up and prepare yourself."

Prepare myself for what? I wondered. Judy sat up and looked me straight in the eye. I thought she was going to say something important.

But she said, "Do I have sleepy dust here?" I checked both of her eyes and said no. I was glad she felt comfortable enough to ask me a personal question like that. But then, as always, I had to go and ruin it all by saying something stupid like, "You know what? Your eyes look a lot prettier today than yesterday."

Yikes. What a dork. If they invented a new bird and called it a 'dork', I'd definitely be one of them. But Judy didn't seem to mind.

In fact, she said, "Why, thank you. That's the nicest thing I've heard all day."

I wasn't sure how to take that either, since we'd both just woken up. She looked embarrassed after saying it, so maybe she was thinking that she was a 'dork' too. A real couple of dorks. That's us. The first of our kind! But at least we had each other.

Over the 'ice speaker' came Mr Crane's voice again. "Would Roy Thrasher and Judy Wren please come to the stage? Roy Thrasher and Judy Wren."

I couldn't believe what I was hearing. Neither could Judy. We pointed at ourselves in astonishment. "Us?"

The crowd surrounding us stepped back to give us room. They were smiling as if we were suddenly something special. I didn't feel special. And I know Judy didn't either. But we'd been given our 'marching orders' and who were we to question them?

Chapter 27

Whiteface

We made our way to the stage. It was about four hundred yards away so it took a long time. And as we approached the stage, I could see Mr Crane looming bigger and bigger.

By the time we were just a few feet away, he seemed huge, towering over us like a giant. He was naturally tall, at least six feet, but being on the stage added another four feet or so, which made his head about ten feet off the ground. That's what I was staring up at, that weird head of his, with those jet-black eyes that don't miss a thing.

He looked down at us with a cockeyed grin. "Why, fancy meeting you here," he said. "Did you enjoy the rest of your detention?" I was just about to ask what happened to him, when he interrupted. "Come around to the back of the stage. Whiteface wants to meet you."

I looked at Judy. "Whiteface? Why would he want to meet us?" Judy shrugged. She seemed excited though. As if suddenly, for once in her life, something good was about to happen.

We did what Mr Crane said. A short distance behind the stage was this kind of round igloo thing, made out of solid blocks of ice. It had a thatched roof on top of it made from bamboo sticks and there was a small wood-burning stove inside that made everything feel cozy.

As we entered, we could see Whiteface. He was bent over, warming his feathers on the stove. He turned around. I couldn't believe how big and round and white his face was. Judy had thought he was a kea, and they're supposed to be pointy-faced and colorful, but he wasn't. It's like all of the color had been drained from his body and all that was left was this pale circle of white and two glittery eyes.

He blinked at me and smiled. "Welcome," he said. "Glad you could make it. Please, sit down."

He motioned Judy and me toward two stools that had been set up on either side of the entrance. "It's a long way to come, isn't it? Especially when you're not used to travelling long distances."

I didn't know how to respond. I cleared my throat and said, "Yes, it's been a long ride. But we're really glad to be here. Really glad. Excited actually." I don't know why I said that. Whiteface cocked his head. He seemed to think it was an odd response. A normal response would have been something like, "What's going on here? What is this? What are we doing here?" But I wanted him to like me.

Judy was more direct. She said, "I thought birds went south in the winter."

Whiteface nodded. "Excellent point, young lady. They normally do. But these are not normal times by any standard. Sometimes sacrifices must be made."

I had no idea what he was talking about. What sacrifices?

"I understand that neither of you have read my book," he said. He held up a copy of "The Last Cycle". Judy felt bad.

"We wished we had. We only heard about it recently. As soon as we get home, we'll get a copy from the library."

Whiteface laughed. "You will not find this book in any library," he said. "Any human library."

He opened up the book and began reading from a chapter. "For every planet, there is a perfect species that outlasts all the others. It is not the strongest. Nor the most intelligent. It is the most adaptable. For Earth, birds are that perfect species. They support each other. They sacrifice themselves so that others may live. They appreciate a good sunset. They fly for pleasure. They do not overeat. They consume to survive and to be happy. Nothing more and nothing less."

Whiteface closed the book with a quiet smile on his face. Judy looked at me. "Wow," she said, "That's really good."

I wasn't as impressed. Not because I disagreed with what he had read. It's just that I didn't know what he was talking about. Why was he talking about 'the perfect species' as being birds?. What was wrong with humans? We seemed to be pretty smart. I mean, if anyone was adaptable, humans were. What about my "Roy Thrasher Earth Suit"? Wasn't that an example of being adaptable?

And electric cars and contact lenses and winter gloves and video games.

Judy noticed a display case lit by candles behind Whiteface. "What's that?" she asked. Whiteface said that inside that case is a sacred text that foretold the future. It was discovered by him five years ago and it was what had inspired him to write "The Last Cycle". It is what guides his life now, and what will guide all birds in the world from here on in.

Judy wanted to take a look at it, but the moment she stood up and moved toward the display case, several other birds got in her way, including Mr Crane.

"Sorry," he said. "Sacred texts aren't for losers." Judy's jaw dropped. I was furious.

Whiteface stepped in. "Now, now. There's no call for that. We're all in this together." But he still wouldn't let us take a look at the sacred text and he wouldn't give us a copy of "The Last Cycle" either. If we hadn't read it by now, he said, it was too late.

Whiteface had a few more things to say. He said Judy and I had been brought here as emissaries from the human world. We are to be part of a special message to all humans. That birds are about to adapt in a way that they had not expected. He wouldn't say what that was, but he did say he was running out of time and that he had more to say to the rest of the crowd, so our meeting here had ended.

With a dismissive wave, Whiteface told Mr Crane that it was time for us to leave. "Thanks for coming," he said. "It's been a pleasure knowing you."

Chapter 28

No Way Out

Mr Crane escorted us out of the ice igloo and back around to the front of the stage. The crowd had cleared a long narrow corridor for us to walk back to where we had been before. But this time, they were quiet as we went by. Judy and I couldn't figure out what was going on.

Once we reached our standing area, the rest of the birds filled in the space and it got noisy again. But they seemed to be keeping one eye on us as if we were something special now that we'd talked to Whiteface personally.

Mr Crane and a few other birds led Whiteface back up onto the stage. The crowd whistled and whooped and hollered. And then got quiet.

Mr Crane put a new graphic up on the giant 'ice screen'. It showed a group of birds and a group of humans. Only the group of birds was much bigger than the group of humans.

"Good morning, everyone," Whiteface bellowed. "Today is a special day. Today, we become what we were always meant to be."

"For every human on this planet," he said, pointing to the chart, "there are six birds. Six bright, wonderful birds of different shapes and colors. Six amazing birds with incredible talents who have come from all over the world and are here right now, listening to what I am saying."

Whiteface nodded toward Mr Crane. Mr Crane stepped forward. He had a bamboo pointing stick in his hand. He pointed up at the ice screen. It reminded me of the time he was teaching in our class. Only this was different. Instead of twenty-five students, now there were millions.

"The average bird weighs approximately two hundred and fifty grams," he said. "The average weight of a human is about sixty kilograms. So, the average human weighs about two hundred and forty times more than the average bird."

Whiteface glared over at him. "Mr Crane, please, get to the point." Mr Crane nodded and cleared his throat.

"As adversaries, humans have a weight advantage. But what we have are the numbers, the individual air mobility, and the element of surprise."

I looked at Judy and whispered, "What the heck is he talking about?"

Judy shrugged back. "I have no idea."

Mr Crane went on. "Now, there are many pockets of vulnerability that humans have not taken into account, such as pecking a hole in a hydraulic hose or flying directly into the engine of an airplane. At five hundred miles an hour, for example, a jet airplane engine produces somewhere between twenty thousand and fifty thousand pounds of thrust…"

Whiteface cut him off. "Mr Crane, that will do!" Mr Crane looked angry at first. And then he nodded. And stepped aside. Whiteface took his place next to the screen.

"What my nerdy assistant here is trying to say, is that what we lack in size and power, we more than make up for in speed and intelligence."

I couldn't take it any more. Were they talking about attacking human beings, like my parents and my brothers? I said to Judy, "This isn't right! I have to say something."

And so, I did. In front of millions of other birds, and Mr Crane, and Whiteface, I spoke up. "Excuse me!" I shouted. "Are you saying you want everyone here to start attacking humans?"

The crowd went super quiet all of a sudden. So quiet that my shrieking voice echoed off the hills surrounding the event. Mr Crane glared at me like he wanted to kill me. Whiteface stepped toward the front of the stage.

"Young man," he said, "We are not attacking anyone. We are defending ourselves and our planet."

My face was red. I didn't know how to respond to that. So, I blurted out, "Prove it."

Whiteface glared at me and said, "I beg your pardon?"

I said, "If you're going to go around attacking people, you need to prove what you're saying. You need to prove that they are attacking you first, otherwise you're just a bully."

Whiteface nodded. A bully, he chuckled. How cute. "Mr Crane, put on the next graphic." Mr Crane switched graphics on the ice screen. What came up were pictures of lakes and rivers covered in oil, rainforests that had been totally clear cut, and freeways that were clogged with cars.

"Humans have been destroying our world. They have been doing it for centuries. And even when it gets pointed out to them by their own kind, they still continue to do it. It is a systematic and deliberate attack against all birds. There is no other way to look at it."

"Yes, there is," I shouted. "Maybe we're still trying to figure it out ourselves, like Thomas Edison did. I bet you've never heard of him, have you?"

"Enough!" Whiteface said.

I looked over at Judy. She was humiliated. Maybe I went too far. It wouldn't have been the first time. But I didn't like what he was saying. The idea of them getting this crowd all worked up just to attack people, like my parents and my brothers, didn't cut it for me.

At that point, Whiteface said to Mr Crane, "Put them in their place."

Uh-oh. That didn't sound good. I looked over at Judy. Her expression sank. I thought maybe we should turn around fly right out of here. Hit the road. Make like a tree and leave. You get the picture. But it was too late.

Judy and I heard a strange whumping sound. We looked up. Four giant cranes, one on each side, were lowering two huge bamboo bird cages down on top of us.

I fluttered around and tried to escape but I was too slow. The pointy parts of the bamboo stuck deep into the icy muck on the ground. Once in place, there was no way to lift them.

Judy pushed with all her weight against the bars. They went nowhere. "I'm stuck!" she shouted. I told her to forget about it, we weren't going anywhere.

Whiteface smiled. "That's right," he said. "You'll be our special little guests until our work is done. So just sit back and enjoy the show. In a week or so, it will all be over."

Some birds in the crowd were cackling as though they were making fun of us. I was furious. "Don't you see what's going on here?" I shouted. "He's put us in a cage. And if he'll put us in a cage, sooner or later, he'll put you in a cage as well."

Chapter 29

Goners

The other birds weren't listening. It's like they didn't see us as birds any more. They were only listening to Mr Crane who had his back to the giant ice screen shrieking instructions.

"Birds of the African continent, go now. Once you reach your home again, travel from house to house. Disconnect the electricity and contaminate the water supply. And then, when people try to escape in their cars, splatter their windshields with everything you've got. Run them off the road!"

With a great WHOOSH! the African birds took off. Wave after wave of them rose up and started heading south.

"South American birds, you are next. Follow the plans laid out in the book. Engage with every human that you can find. Show them who is the dominant species. Wake them up if they are asleep. If they are riding bicycles, force them off the road. If they are walking, scare them back into their apartments. If they are cooking, sever their power cables and throws rocks at their windows."

And then came China and Southeast Asia. Judy and I listened, and watched, as great waves of birds took flight. None of it made any sense to me. What had humans done to them? I mean, besides polluting the water and destroying their eating grounds. It's not like we did it on purpose.

Canada, U.S., and Mexico, they were the last to go. I guess because they were the closest.

Chickens and penguins were all that remained. Since they couldn't fly, or just barely, at least, Mr Crane ordered them to set up communication centers. They'd be the transmitters of information, branch managers who could monitor how well the attacks were going. I was surprised by how gung-ho the penguins were. I used to think of them as funny little birds in tuxedos. Not any more.

At the very end, there was just a few stragglers. Confused looking birds who didn't seem to know where to go or what to do. They would wander around on the ground and bump into each other. Not every bird is a self-motivated genius like Whiteface or good with numbers like Mr Crane. Some are just ordinary. Like Judy and me.

At the end of the launch day, they turned off the stage lights and everything went quiet. Judy and I were still stuck in our cages. And still wondering why we had been singled out.

Whiteface must have known we were humans all along. I mean, why else would he say we were 'emissaries to the human world.' Did he mean we were birds who were supposed to send messages to humans, or that we were humans who had been turned into birds, who were supposed to send messages to humans?

My head was spinning. And frankly, I didn't care any more what Whiteface was thinking. I only thought about Judy and how worried she was and what I could do to make her feel better.

She'd been quiet a long time. She was slumped down in her cage. I couldn't tell if she was asleep or not. Or even if she was sick or something.

"Hey, Judy?" I whispered.

"Yeah", she said.

"You okay?" I asked.

"Yeah," she said.

I nodded to myself. There was a long pause. I couldn't tell what she was thinking.

"What do you think they're going to do to us?" she said.

"I don't know," I responded.

"Do you think they were always planning to put us in these cages?" she asked.

I had no idea.

"Did you see how everyone was looking at us," she said. "Like we were criminals?"

I could tell from her voice that she was almost crying. I think, with the exception of that detention at school, she'd never been in trouble before.

I was about to say something, just to try and make her feel better, when she said, "I want to go home."

I didn't know how to respond to that. I wanted to go home too. But I didn't want to say that because I wanted to appear strong. That seemed to be the best thing to do. But let's face it, home seemed about as far away from here as you can get.

If my parents could see me now, I wondered what they would have said. My dad would probably have said something like, "Good old Roy, always getting himself in a pickle." I never understood what being in a pickle meant. I don't like pickles. And even if I did, what would be the point of being inside one of them?

After a while, Judy fell asleep. I could hear someone snoring behind the stage. I assumed it was Mr Crane. With that long throat of his, I bet he can really rip out the sounds at night. Eventually, I fell asleep too. But for how long, who knows?

Not long enough, obviously, because, in the middle of the night, there was this strange little tap-tap-tapping sound on the bamboo bars of my cage. I tried to ignore it but it kept going on and on.

I opened my eyes. I couldn't see anyone. I looked around. Nothing. Then I heard it again. Tap-tap-tap.

And then a tiny voice said, "Hey!"

I looked down. There was a small, dark face looking up at me. "How's it going?" it said.

It was Rio. I was really happy to see him. For a few seconds anyway. And then I remembered how he'd taken off on Judy and me back at the school grounds. "Not real great," I said. The understatement of a lifetime.

"Well, it's not going to get any better," he said. "They've got plans for you."

I looked at him. "What do you mean, plans?"

Rio sighed. "You really haven't read the book, have you. The Last Migration?"

I shrugged. No, I haven't. "What do I care about the migration of a bunch of birds?"

Rio shook his head. "It's not the last migration of birds, you dodo. It's the last migration of humans."

I didn't know what he was talking about. And I didn't know what a 'dodo' was, but it didn't sound very nice.

"Look, birds migrate," he said. "That's what we do. It's what we've always done. When things get tough, we take off. It's humans that refuse to migrate. They're the ones who would rather change everything around them than migrate."

"So, that's what humans do. So what?" I said.

Rio leaned closer. He had an intense look on his face. "So, The Last Migration means…" He drew a finger across his throat and made a sound like it was a knife.

"…the end for humans. No more. Finis. Lights out. And the birds are going to make sure it happens."

My mouth dropped. "What about us? Do they have plans for us," I asked. "For me and Judy?"

Rio shook his head. "I just wished you'd read the book. Then you wouldn't have come here."

"What do you mean, we wouldn't have come here?" I asked. "Why wouldn't we have come here?"

"Because," he said, "you guys are supposed to be…" He stopped abruptly. He had a dark look on his face.

"What?" I asked.

"Sacrificed," he said.

"What?!" I whispered loudly, trying to keep my voice down. "What do you mean, sacrificed??"

Rio said it was all right there, in black and white, in the book, "The Last Cycle". Two humans were supposed to be turned into birds and then sacrificed for good luck before the last cycle begins.

"Why didn't you tell us?" I asked.

Rio shrugged. I could tell that he felt bad. "I was sworn to secrecy," he said. "I was hoping that you'd have read the book by now and then maybe you would have just taken off."

Wow. What a guy. And what's the deal with writing a book about something and then everybody suddenly has to do what it says? Since when did that become a law?

It was about that time that I wished I was one of those people who was a bigger reader. Some people read every book they can get their hands on. Not me. But then again, I'd never even heard of "The Last Cycle" until a few hours ago, so it wouldn't have made any difference. The whole thing felt like some kind of a trick.

Rio could see that I was upset. I mean, wouldn't you be? How's that going to look like on my tombstone. "Here lies Roy Archibald Thrasher. A decent guy. Sacrificed by a bunch of birds." Who'd want to visit a grave like that?

There was a noise from somewhere behind the stage. Rio looked over. He got worried.

"Look," he said, "I'm on your side. Just hang tough and I'll be back. Don't go anywhere!" He disappeared.

Chapter 30

The Belly Plot

Where was I going to go? Disneyland? My head was spinning. Why didn't I see this? It was like some board game, and Judy and I were two pieces being moved around.

I thought about everything that had happened since we got here. Being brought backstage into Whiteface's tent. Mr Crane being rude. Seeing The Last Cycle book for the first time. And that display case at the back of the room.

That display case. Why wouldn't they let us see that? What was in there? I was trying to remember.

"Judy," I whispered loudly. "Judy!"

Judy woke up. She rubbed her eyes with her wings. "What?"

"What was in that display case at the back of the room," I asked.

"What room," she said. She was still half asleep.

"Whiteface's room. Behind the stage. What was in that display case?"

"How would I know," she said.

"You asked Whiteface and he said something. What did he say?" Judy shrugged.

I didn't want to tell her what Rio had said about the sacrificing and all that because I thought it might put her over the edge, you know, emotionally. I was over the edge already so it was too late for me.

Then, suddenly, she remembered.

"He said it was a sacred text that he discovered that foretold the future," she said. "He said it was the whole reason he wrote his book."

A plan was starting to gel in my tiny bird brain. We needed to find out where Whiteface got that text from and what was in it. If he was basing every single thing that he was doing on that, then we needed to know what it said.

"One of us has to sneak back in there and read that text," I said. Judy gave me a look that was halfway between "No way!" and "What are you, some kind of idiot?"

I couldn't blame her. I didn't think it was a good idea either. But it was the only one that I had.

And then I remembered seeing this movie once, where this prisoner pretends to be sick, and he gets taken to the prison hospital, where he meets this nurse and they end up falling in love and she helps him escape.

Now, I had no intention of falling in love with Whiteface or, heaven forbid, Mr Crane. But I did see it as a way of getting in there and reading that so-called 'sacred text'.

I told my plan to Judy. She didn't like it at first. But then she shrugged and said, "What do we have to lose?" I was about to tell her that we stood to lose everything, but then I caught myself. One person over the edge was enough.

Now, I've had belly aches as a human before, and I know what they are like, so I thought it should be me. Judy agreed. So, we gave it a go. I started moaning and sobbing and holding my belly. Only nobody came. So, I moaned louder and louder.

Judy noticed something. "Listen! The snoring has stopped!" she said. Which meant Mr Crane was probably awake. I kept moaning and groaning and rolling around on the ground and I even picked up some mud and rubbed it near my butt so it looked like I was pooping. It was a real soap opera.

The stage lights turned on. Mr Crane appeared from around the back of the stage. He had an irritated look on his face.

He waddled toward Judy and me and said, "Now what?"

I looked him square in those beady little eyes of his and lied. "It's my stomach," I said. "It's really bad. I feel like I could be a goner any minute!"

Mr Crane rolled his eyes. And with no sincerity at all he said, "Well, we wouldn't want that now, would we? Hold on."

He shook his head and disappeared around the back of the stage. He reappeared a few minutes later. "Turns out

Whiteface wants to talk to you two anyway. It's getting near that time."

Getting near that time? Yikes. I noticed a faint light in the sky. Maybe sunrise was when they were going to do us in.

Two large, nasty-looking penguins appeared alongside Mr Crane. The two penguins lifted up the edges of our two cages and that allowed us to squeeze out. We followed the penguins back around the stage and into Whiteface's igloo.

There were two doves who looked like nurses standing next to Whiteface. They had masks on their faces. Whiteface watched as they helped me onto the bed. They started to examine me, checking around my stomach for what the problem was.

Meanwhile, Judy faded into the background, moving quietly around toward the display case. I groaned extra loudly, then shouted out in pain. That got everyone's attention.

Judy took the opportunity to lift up the top of the display case. She removed what looked like a single page from an old newspaper. Only some of the words on the page had other words pasted on top of them. Judy scanned the article and gave me a confused look. She then quickly put it back into the display case before anyone could see.

A moment later, I stopped my moaning. I looked at the two doves. "Wow, you guys are incredible. I feel so much better now!" They said they hadn't done anything. I disagreed. "Whatever you did with all that cooing and those wonderful wings of yours, that was magic." They looked at their wings with surprise.

Whiteface had seen enough. "Great. Off you go then. And try not to be any more trouble. You only have a few more days."

The two penguins walked us back to our cages. I felt a mix of relief and dread. Relieved to be away from Whiteface and Mr Crane. But dreading what was to come next.

The penguins lifted up the two sides of the cages and pushed us back in. "Thanks for the friendly service," I said. "How about some apple pie and ice cream?" I don't know why I said that, but it was just stupid enough to make Judy laugh, and so as far as I was concerned, it was all worthwhile.

Someone turned the stage lights off again. The sun was rising so it didn't make much difference. I was just happy to have a few days left. And be able to share them with Judy.

"What was in the case?" I whispered. Judy shushed me. She was worried the penguins could hear us.

"I'll tell you later," she said.

I whispered back, 'Don't make it too much later or it won't matter'.

Chapter 31

Judy Gets the Bad News

We both fell asleep. When we woke up, the sun was shining. The place was empty. And pretty much every bird was gone.

Judy motioned me toward the edge of her cage. "It was a newspaper clipping," she whispered, "taken from page thirty-two of some newspaper". I couldn't figure out what she was talking about. "Some of the words had been replaced with other words, you know, like a ransom note."

"What did it say?" I asked. Judy shrugged.

"It said, 'Three Cycles... Of Birds... The Last Cycle... Get Rid Of... Humans... Forever.' And there were these numbers scratched across the top: '849 U.S' and '195 Canada'. And then at the bottom were the words, 'Never again' and 'Save The Planet'.

I looked at Judy. What's that supposed to mean? She shrugged. "The paper was really old and yellow," she said. "At the very top was the date: October 13, 2011." I asked her if she could tell where the newspaper came from and she said no.

I thought about it for a while. "We've got to find that original newspaper before it was changed," I said. "We've got to figure out what this whole thing means."

A short while later, Rio wandered by. He was good at keeping a low profile. He leaned toward our two cages. "Word has it you guys have five more days." I tried to shush him but it was too late.

Judy had heard what he'd said. "Rio? Five more days before what?"

Rio glared at me, "You mean, you haven't told her?" I sighed. Talk about a small bird with a big mouth.

"No," I said. I figured there was no point.

Rio suddenly got what I was saying. "Oops. Sorry."

Judy kept at me. "Tell me what's going on?" I had to tell her what Rio had told me. That if we had read The Last Cycle, we'd have known that we were to be sacrificed.

Judy's heart sank. "So that's what this was all about. Why the two of us were chosen to meet Whiteface over everybody else. Why our two wishes were granted. And why Rio and Old Crow and the others had brought us here in the first place."

"Okay," Rio said. "I know it's a shock. But you've got to listen to me, okay?" But Judy had heard enough. Why should she listen to anything more that he had to say?

Rio said, "Not all of us are on board with this, do you understand? There is a group of us that don't like what's happening. We don't think humans are to blame for everything. And we don't think that humans aren't trying to make things better. It's just that, it's just that… and don't take this the wrong way, you're kind of dim-witted and slow."

Judy didn't want to hear this. But I did. "You mean to say that there's like an underground."

Rio said no. It's very much above ground. "But it's secret," he said. I asked him what plans this 'above ground' had to stop Whiteface.

Rio shook his head. "That's the problem," he said. "We don't have a plan. Plus, there are too many of them and not enough of us. And they'll believe anything that Whiteface tells them."

I looked over at Judy. She was still reacting to the idea of being sacrificed. But my head was exploding with ideas.

"Listen to me," I said to Rio. "I need to send a message to my brothers."

Rio thought I was nuts. "What for?"

"Because we're almost out of time. And they can get to the bottom of what The Last Cycle is all about. We need to know where that "sacred text" came from."

Judy shook her head. "What's the point?" she said. "Any message we send from here won't get there for days. By then it will be too late."

Rio disagreed. "We've got carrier pigeons. They fly all night. They can be anywhere in forty-eight hours."

Judy wasn't sure. But I was. We could do this, I thought. We just had to believe it could happen.

"Listen," I said to Judy, "Our whole lives, the two of us have thought we were losers. Up until this moment."

Judy wasn't sure what I was driving at.

"It doesn't matter if this works," I said. "The thing is, we have to try. That's the difference between being a loser and not being a loser. We have to try."

I know, I know. I was getting all inspirational and everything. But I really did believe in what I was saying.

A moment passed. I must have gotten through to Judy because her face brightened all of a sudden. And then she said to me, "What are you thinking about?"

I told her that my parents were useless. And that my brothers may be complete idiots, but at least they know how to work the Internet. And that's what we needed right now. Two idiots who know how to work the Internet.

Judy and I helped Rio write out five separate but identical notes to my brothers. We figured that if two or three of the carrier pigeons got lost or didn't make it for some reason, the third, fourth, or fifth would probably get there.

Within minutes, Rio was gone. And with him, our plan for stopping this madness.

All that was left now was to wait. And hope Whiteface and Mr Crane or the penguins didn't figure out what we were doing.

Chapter 32

Attack

The first wave of birds reached North Africa three days after Whiteface gave the signal. They landed in Morocco and Tunisia and Algeria.

It made the news all over the world. At first, people were delighted that the birds were back again.

But then, when the birds started chewing on electrical wires and sending rocks through people's windows and running them off roads, that all changed pretty quickly.

Reporters and scientists tried to figure out what was going on. When did birds start behaving in such an 'un-bird-like' manner? Was it something in the air or water that was making them crazy? Was there a solar flare or an earthquake that set them off?

They soon figured out that it wasn't just some random series of events. It was coordinated. And it wasn't just happening in North Africa either. Pretty soon, it had spread all the way down to the Congo, Uganda, Kenya, and even South Africa.

A day or so later, every country in Europe came under attack. And then South America and Asia. And finally, by day three, North America.

At times like this, humans have a habit of turning to so-called experts for explanations. But the experts were as clueless as everyone else. And the news broadcasts just made it worse. Fear was everywhere.

My mother was totally freaked out. She knocked over her teacup when she found out that the attacks had started to spread to North America.

She and my dad were glued to the TV from dawn to dusk. They watched the news and then stood by the window keeping an eye out. My brother, Ryan, pointed out that there had been local reports of birds hurling rocks through glass, so they'd better keep back.

Spencer wasn't worried. He was still sneaking out after dinner to visit his girlfriend. He'd say things like, "Why should I worry about a bunch of birds?" and "Who's bigger, me or them? I've got the weight advantage."

But then, one evening, the electricity went out and everybody got scared. There's nothing like being in total darkness to grab your attention.

My dad promised to go out and get a generator the next day. But when he called the Home Depot, the guy just laughed.

He said, "Take a number, buddy. There are five hundred and sixty-nine customers ahead of you." My dad didn't like the tone of the guy's voice so he checked around at some other stores, but nobody had a generator.

So, he bought candles. Birthday candles. Every one that he could find. There must have been enough candles in the bucket that he brought home to cover the next million birthdays. They didn't give off a ton of light but at least they made my mother feel better.

She said, "We might as well celebrate a few birthdays while we're at it since we're going to be burning the candles anyway".

The electricity wasn't cut off for long. The power crews were pretty good at fixing the wires. They knew that birds had been chewing on them. They just didn't know how they had managed to break the wires entirely.

Had they been able to monitor all of the wires all of the time, they would have seen the moment when hundreds of birds stood on each side of the chewed-out part. The birds would bounce up and down, over and over again, until the wires finally snapped. That's birds for you. When they get something in their little minds, they don't give up.

True to his word, Rio sent the carrier pigeons off with the messages. And true to their word, the carrier pigeons made it to their destinations in less than forty-eight hours.

They had the address. They just didn't know what Ryan and Spencer looked like. So, they hovered around in circles over the top of the house waiting for somebody to come out.

Eventually, my dad walked outside to get into his car. He was going to try and pick up a pizza that he'd ordered from Me 'n Ed's Pizza, which was about six blocks away.

He had just started the engine when a rock fell from somewhere above and cracked the windshield. He started shouting, "Great. As if things aren't bad enough!"

Ryan noticed him pacing around outside. He went out to see what was wrong. My dad said some idiot threw a rock at his windshield. Ryan looked up. Four birds were circling overhead. Spencer came outside. He saw Ryan looking skyward.

"What's going on?" he asked.

Ryan was just about to answer, when one of the pigeons dropped another rock and it hit him right on the forehead. "Ow! What the heck!" Spencer started to chuckle, until a third rock hit him on the head. The last rock fell onto the roof somewhere and rolled into a gutter.

Spencer picked up the rock that hit him from the ground. "Look, it's wrapped in some kind of note." Ryan and my dad gazed up at the sky. The five birds were still circling around overhead. They picked up the two rocks that were also wrapped in notes.

Spencer unwrapped his rock and read the note. "Don't throw this away. It's me, Roy."

Spencer couldn't believe it. "Dad! It's from Roy!"

Dad and Ryan ran over.

Spencer kept reading. "It says 'Don't worry about where I am. I need you guys to do me a favor. Go on the Internet and look up all the newspapers you can find from October 13, 2011. If there is anything, any article, that has the words, "The Last Cycle" and "Never Again" and the numbers 849 and 195, clip the whole thing out and send it to me. Do it now." Ryan and Dad checked the notes on their rocks and they said the same thing.

Ryan shrugged. "Hey, at least the guy's still alive."

My dad accused Ryan of being a dull tool and told him, "What are you waiting for? Get to work!"

He pushed him toward the house. Now, my dad never pushed anybody, at least anybody I ever saw. So, when he pushed Ryan, both he and Spencer ran into the house fast and got to work. A few minutes later, my dad got the ladder out and climbed up onto the roof to look for that fifth rock.

I wished I could have seen Ryan and Spencer scouring the Internet. It would have been hilarious. I mean, serious, but hilarious at the same time.

Those two have never worked on anything together, let alone try to save me, or, for that matter, the entire world. But they didn't know what was at stake, which was probably a good thing because neither of them do well under pressure. I mean, the reason they both failed grade five was because they would freeze up at the very sound of the word 'test'. Ryan was the only kid I ever heard of that had an ulcer at age nine. Mind you, eating potato chips and salsa all the time probably didn't help either.

Chapter 33

Ryan and Spencer Get Cracking

Judy and I waited. What choice did we have? With all of the other birds gone, it felt like we were the last two customers at a rock concert that finished a long time ago. Which, in a way, was kind of true. But it didn't make things any easier to think of it that way.

There was this creepy quiet and a pretty bad smell. Along with all of these loose feathers that kept blowing around in the shape of whirlwinds.

And then, I think it was the third day after all the birds had left, that Mr Crane and the penguins reappeared. They were carrying twigs and branches and buckets full of dried leaves from who knows where. They'd dump them all in the middle of the stage and then waddle off again.

Judy and I would look at each other and wonder what was going on. And then, just around sunset on the third day, they started lashing together these bamboo poles and building this thing that looked like a tent that stood over the top of the twigs and branches. I remember thinking, 'Man, if these guys had been in the boy scouts, there is no way they would have gotten any of the badges that I got'.

And then, suddenly, it dawned on me. I looked over at Judy. She wasn't seeing what I was seeing, which was probably a good thing. Because what I was seeing was eventually supposed to turn us into goners.

They were planning to build a giant bonfire on stage. And then they were going to lash something, or somebody, to those bamboo poles and watch the whole thing burn. Guess who that was supposed to be?

I tried to keep Judy from seeing what was happening. I'd talk to her about school and growing up and our parents and brothers and sisters. Anything to keep her mind from putting two and two together. I'd say things like, "You think those notes got through? Geez, what if they don't?"

I reminded her that it was our best shot. That Rio had a lot of confidence in the carrier pigeons. And that my brothers might not be the sharpest knives in the drawer but they did know how to work the Internet.

"I'm pretty sure they can do it," I said, "At least I hope they can." But I didn't know. Nobody knew. Not even them.

Around that time, back home, my dad was sitting my mom down in the kitchen and telling her the news. My mom nearly fainted. She started to cry.

"Oh, thank God," she said. "I always knew he was alive!" She didn't always know that. But that's what adults say sometimes. I guess it makes them feel smarter or something.

My mom thought they should go to the police right away. My dad reminded her the police hadn't done much lately, and that they are probably not going to do much now just because some birds dropped a few rocks on our heads.

"No, we should just do what the notes say," he said. "Ryan and Spencer are working on it right now." That didn't make my mom feel any better. "It's the internet," my dad said. "They're way better at it than we are." That was true. But it wasn't much comfort to my mom.

Ryan and Spencer were on their computers. Their bedrooms were opposite each other in the hallway so they could talk through the open doorway. Ryan, being the oldest, took charge.

"You take the local papers," he shouted, "I'm going national."

"Okay," Spencer said. "But this is insane." Ryan told him to just do it.

Spencer went to the websites of two local newspapers, "The Northside Gazette" and "The Evening Tattler". Neither was very big, and most of their pages were filled with advertising and local gossip. Ryan went onto "The Globe" website and an international paper called "Western Hemisphere News".

They each found an Oct. 13, 2011 edition of one of the papers at the same time. Spencer yelled out, "Got one!"

"Me too!" shouted Ryan.

It was exactly at that time that the power went out. The house went dark. And their screens went blank. I don't have to tell you what my brothers said at that moment. But my mother told them to wash out their mouths.

The power outage seemed to last an eternity. As it turned out, three blocks away, a giant flock of herons had pelted a power transformer with rocks. Something on the inside got disconnected from something on the outside and there was this giant shower of sparks, and that's when the power went out.

My dad ran out into the street to see what was going on. None of the other houses had power. Overhead, the same five carrier pigeons were hovering around in a circle.

Meanwhile, inside, my mom was hovering over Ryan's computer screen. "Come on, come on."

Ryan said, "Mom, just wishing something could happen isn't going to make it happen."

Just then, the power came back on. "Yes!" my mother said, giving Ryan an 'I told you so' look. Ryan rolled his eyes. And got back to work. He brought up the Oct. 13th edition of The Globe and started to scan the news articles for the words "The Last Cycle" and "Never Again". Nothing. Ryan and my mother slumped.

Spencer was busy scanning The Northside Gazette for the same words. None of the articles had any of those words in them except for 'Local recycling days have been changed".

"I'm not getting anything," he shouted.

Ryan shook his head. "There's nothing in here," he said.

My mother wasn't giving up. "What about the advertising? Have you looked at the advertising?"

Ryan thought she was being ridiculous. "Who's going to use those words in some advertisement?" My mother insisted he try it anyway.

Ryan set the scan to include 'advertising'. He pressed the 'search' button and… WHAM! There it was. In an ad for dishwashers. The words weren't in sequence, but they were there.

The ad said, "Is your dishwasher not doing what it's supposed to do? Our final dishwashing cycle, THE LAST CYCLE, is called 'Total Clean' and it means it! NEVER AGAIN suffer the humiliation of dirty dishes!"

My mother shouted, "There!" Ryan's jaw dropped. He couldn't believe what he was seeing. Spencer came up with the same advertisement in the "Northside Gazette" and "The Evening Tattler". It was for a dishwasher called "Electro-Clean" and it was made in Europe. Germany, to be exact.

Ryan scanned all the newspapers for that same advertisement on that same day. Turns out the ad had been placed in 849 U.S. newspapers and 195 Canadian newspapers. His face turned white. He turned to my mom.

"Mom, I'm probably never going to say this again in my entire life but you're a genius." My mother smiled.

He told Spencer to quit looking. He found what they were looking for. What it means, he has no idea. But at least they had it. Now they had to figure out how to get the information back to Roy, wherever he was.

Chapter 34

A Billion to One

They didn't know it, but I was in exactly the same place I'd been in for days. Stuck in a birdcage way up north. But I have to admit, I was starting to lose my confidence. And when that goes, watch out. Because you can bring everyone down with you.

I started thinking about the bonfire and the sacrifice and how much time we had left. And that, somehow, it was my fault that Judy was stuck here with me.

If I had just said to her in our detention, 'Let's run away', we wouldn't have made that stupid wish and ended up here. Or if I'd talked to her in the hallway instead of ignoring her. Or if I'd done any one of a million things differently than what I had done, none of this would have happened.

I started to feel down. "Look," I said, "I don't think my brothers are going to get that message. The odds are a billion to one."

Judy said, "What do you mean?"

I said, "Even if all of those pigeons make it there, what are the odds that my brothers will even get the message? I mean, they're totally clueless."

I started to apologize for wrecking everything. "This is ridiculous," I said. "It's never going to change. I'm always going to be like this, right up to the end."

Judy said, "Be like what?"

And then I said it. Those two dumb words. "A loser."

Judy went silent. She didn't say a word. Nothing. I could barely see her face in the dark shadows of her cage. Finally, she said something. Only it was really quiet.

"Well, I'm not."

I couldn't hear her. I asked her to repeat what she'd said.

She said, "Well, I'm not. I'm not a loser. And if you think you are, then we can't be together."

I went completely silent. I could barely breathe. I didn't know what to say. I sat in my cage, like a defeated little bird and said absolutely nothing. And if that isn't the sign of a loser, I don't know what is.

Meanwhile, back home, my dad called a family meeting. He laid out all of the possibilities. As it turned out, there weren't any. "We don't know where he is. We don't know how to get this message to him. And we don't know what will happen if we don't get the message to him."

Now, I have to admit, my mother isn't usually one to come up with the ideas. But she came up with two doozies in a row.

Because, right then, she said, "Where are those birds that brought these messages here in the first place?"

My dad and my brothers looked at each other. They raced outside and gazed up into the sky. Sure enough, the carrier pigeons were still there, only they were circling so high that you could barely see them now.

A few minutes later, my dad and my brothers lined up the same five rocks on the road out front of our house with new messages on tiny pieces of paper that they had written on each of them.

And then they waited. And waited. And waited. They kept looking up. But the carrier pigeons weren't doing anything. They just kept flying around overhead.

My mother yelled out from the front door. "Here! Put some of this out for them." She had taken a piece of leftover roast beef from our Sunday dinner a few days ago and cut it up into five equal pieces.

Spencer raced over and got the meat. He ran back to the five rocks and dropped the meat next to each one of them. Then stepped back.

Almost immediately, the carrier pigeons started to drop down from the sky. They were like rockets. They must have dropped five hundred feet in ten seconds.

Each of them swooped down. They landed right in front of the meat. And then gobbled it up quickly.

If I'd been there, now that I'm a bird, I would have been able to see those pigeons smile and nod, but my family couldn't. They didn't have my trained eye.

But they did watch in silence as the pigeons picked up the rocks, one after another, and took back off into the sky.

My family let out a cheer. "Yeah!" they all yelled. Even my mother jumped up and down and pumped her fist into the air, and that had to be a first.

It had been over an hour since I made that fateful decision of calling myself a loser in front of Judy. I couldn't take her silence any more. I had to know what was going on in her head. Although I had a pretty good idea.

"Could we at least talk about this?" I asked.

"What for?" Judy replied.

"Because we should at least talk to one another."

Judy said she didn't see why. I'd already given up on everything, so what's the point?

I said I hadn't given up on her.

"Well, I've given up on you," she said. "So, whatever happens from here on in, I now know that I'm on my own."

I said that wasn't true. I was with her all the way.

She said, "Why would I want to be with someone who thinks they're a loser at a time like this?"

I went quiet. She had a point. Who would want to be with someone who thought they were a loser at any time? What good is it going to do them? And then I wondered what it was in my head that was making me think those thoughts because, deep down inside, I didn't believe they were true.

"I'm not a loser," I said.

Judy snapped back, "Sure you are. Look at you."

I moved to the edge of my cage. "No, I'm not."

And she said, "Yes, you are."

We went back and forth like that for a while. And we said it quicker and quicker and quicker, until our words collided in a giant mishmash of the word 'loser'. And then we stopped.

Judy laughed.

I didn't know what she was laughing about. Was she laughing at me? But then, as I watched her, I started to laugh too. There we were, two birds in cages who were about to be turned into crispy critters, laughing our heads off. Now, does that make any sense?

Well, of course, it doesn't. Nothing was making sense except for two things. Judy and I weren't losers. And we were going to do whatever it took to stop Whiteface and his gang from taking over.

Chapter 35

This Means War

The carrier pigeons flew non-stop and they flew fast. I guess my mom's pot roast arrived at the perfect time for them. Within twenty-four hours, they had already passed through the Crow's Nest Pass and were heading down out onto the great plains.

At one point, it looked like two of them had gotten lost, but it just turned out they'd stopped for water.

Time was running out quickly. A lot of the birds had returned from their first battles against the humans and were getting ready for their second. I could tell they were in good spirits because they were boasting about their victories. I overheard one group say, "We cut off their power supply in less than fifteen minutes. Humans were in chaos. They were running around in the streets and that's when we hit them with everything we had. Splat!" They all laughed.

They sat around waiting for further instructions from Mr Crane and Whiteface. A few seagulls wandered over to our two cages and looked inside. "What happened to you?" one scoffed. "Did you get another detention?"

I said, sort of, but that's not why we're here. "We're here because we found out what all of you have been doing is wrong. Humans aren't the enemies. They don't want to destroy us. And we shouldn't be attacking them."

They didn't want to hear that. And without evidence, who can blame them? All they had to go on was what Whiteface was saying and what was written in his book, The Last Cycle. And now, here were two pint-sized, formerly human, birds, who had never fought for anything in their lives, mouthing off about their war.

The more birds that arrived, the more I could see that the timing of the sacrifice probably wasn't far off.

Sure enough, Rio returned with more news. A penguin told him that Whiteface has changed his mind. He wanted to do the sacrifice a day early because the birds had been returning sooner than he'd thought. They were getting ready to go out again and he wanted to celebrate before they left.

Celebrate? How could anyone think that getting rid of Judy and me could be a celebration?

Nevertheless, I knew what he meant. It meant that, if the carrier pigeons didn't make it back by sunset tonight, it would be all over for Judy and me.

Rio felt crummy about giving us the bad news. And we felt crummy about getting it. But at least we knew where we stood. We had less than twelve hours to find a way out of this mess and that was that. As my dad used to say, there's the way that you want things to be, and then there's the way they are, and never the twain shall meet. I never understood the 'twain' part of that but I got the rest. Maybe you can figure it out.

Back home, there wasn't a lot my family could do except hang around and worry. Ryan and Spencer had no idea what that newspaper ad was all about. My mother thought I might have left home and become a dishwasher salesman. My dad thought that was ridiculous but he didn't have any better explanation to offer.

They talked about whether to tell Mr and Mrs Wren. My dad thought they should wait a while. The stuff with the pigeons would only get them all confused, and Mrs Wren didn't look like she could stand much more confusion. I mean, holding that séance was bad enough. Getting messages from the bird world might put her over the edge.

So, they waited and watched all the breaking news on television. All over the world, birds were wreaking havoc. In Morocco, a soccer team had been pummeled by pelicans who had broken into a candy store and filled their beaks up with jawbreakers. In Paris, a family of American tourists riding on bicycles along the Seine River were knocked over the side and nearly drowned. In Vancouver harbor, the cruise ships had been pelted with so much poop that nobody wanted to step outside on the decks.

All over the United States, power grids were damaged and cellphone towers were toppled so that cellphones weren't working any more. People started to panic. And government officials had no idea what to do.

Spencer remembered the note that had been dropped off on the front porch, the one from the bluebird of happiness. He guessed that our wish hadn't come true.

"I knew it. It was all a bunch of bunk anyway," he said.

My mother didn't like it when someone talked that way. "You don't know that," she said to Spencer. "It still might come true."

Spencer rolled his eyes. "Look at the news, Mom," he said. "The world's falling apart."

There was no arguing about that. But my mom also had a point. "It's never over till the fat lady sings," she said.

My brothers looked at her like she was nuts. "What's that supposed to mean?" they said at exactly the same time. It was just one of those weird expressions that old people have. You have to think that it meant something to somebody at some time and just leave it at that.

News reporters said that the armies of the world couldn't figure out how to handle things. They're used to attacking one enemy at a time and usually in one place.

With the birds, they were everywhere all at once and they were silent. You could track them with radar but their groups were so small and they'd split up and then regroup so quickly that you couldn't do anything about it. And by the time you'd responded to one attack, they were already gone and doing another one.

One four-star general said, "I've been in a lot of battles before, on land and in the air, but nothing like this. These birds are driving us crazy."

I'd been sitting in my cage, watching Judy. Making sure she was okay. She kept staring at the sky. Watching the sun sink closer and closer to the horizon. I knew what she was thinking because I was thinking the same thing. We were down to minutes now. Not hours.

"Hey, Judy?" I said. "We are going to get out of this."

She looked at me. "You don't know that," she said. Then she sighed. "I want to write a message to my parents."

I looked around at our two cages. There was nothing to write on. I could see one of the penguins standing with his back to us.

"Excuse me?" The penguin turned around. "Do you have any paper?" The penguin gave me a 'don't bug me' look. I turned back to Judy, "You see what being nice can do for you?" I was joking of course. I decided to take a different approach.

"Hey, numbskull!" I shouted. "It just so happens that we know Whiteface. Personally. And if you want to keep your pathetic stupid job, you'd better find us some paper and fast!"

The guy didn't move at first. But then I think what I said finally got to him and he toddled off. Penguins. Everybody loves them, but they're not much different from any other bird. They're not colorful. And they can't even fly, so there you go.

The penguin returned a few minutes later with a piece of crumpled-up paper and a chewed-down-to-the-eraser pencil that he must have found in Whiteface's hut.

"Give it to her," I said, motioning to Judy.

The penguin tossed the paper and pencil into Judy's cage. "Now quit bugging me, the both of you," he grumbled.

He turned and left. Judy looked at me and smiled.

"Thank you," she said. She picked up the piece of paper and smoothed it out with her feathers.

"What are you going to write?" I asked.

Judy shrugged. "I just want them to know that I was here and that I was thinking about them all the way to the end."

I nodded. That seemed right. I should have done the same thing except there wasn't enough paper and I didn't want to interrupt her. Besides, she'd thought of it first. So, I sat down and kept quiet. And waited.

Then I looked over at her. She was staring at me. She hadn't written a word. She said, "I'm sorry for what I said earlier. I was scared. You're not a loser. You're the opposite of that. You're brave and kind. And I always want to be with you."

Wow! Did I hear that right? Because, if I did, that was the best thing anyone has ever said to me in my entire life. I thought I shouldn't say anything back to her just in case I got it wrong or screwed it up. I'd just let those golden words hang there for a while and savor them, like a really good sandwich.

Judy started scribbling on the piece of paper. When she was finished, she folded it up carefully into a little packet. She then leaned down and pecked a small hole in the ground and dropped it inside. She covered the hole with dirt and then plucked one of her own feathers and stuck it in the ground, pointy side down, to mark the spot.

"Did you see where I put this?" she said. I nodded. "Good," she said, "because, you know, maybe only one of us makes it through and then the other will know where it is."

I remember thinking that if it was just me that made it, I wouldn't want to be around without her. But I didn't tell her that because I thought it might upset her.

I heard noises coming from the back of the stage. And saw the shadows of penguins moving things around. Mr Crane was shouting at them to quit being so clumsy and to hurry up because Whiteface would be here soon.

I don't think Judy heard that because she didn't react or say anything. She was watching the sun, which was barely above the horizon now, poking its way down. Ticking off the last few minutes of daylight, and probably us.

Chapter 36

The Sacrifice

Who knew where the carrier pigeons were? As far as Judy and I could tell, they had probably gotten lost and were hanging out in Mexico somewhere drinking pina coladas.

The moment the sun set, a shiver ran up my spine. Darkness fell quickly across the tundra. I looked up. There were stars overhead. The air was super cold.

On the stage, the penguins were scurrying about. Mr Crane brought out a weird-looking box about the size of a loaf of bread. Inside, I could see a flickering light.

I knew instantly what it was for. He and the penguins were going to use it to start the bonfire. But how did they ever figure out a way to create fire? And when did birds ever use fire anyway? They never needed it up until now. I shrugged it off. I figured by the time I had the answers to those questions it would be too late anyway.

Whiteface poked his head out to look at the crowd. It was a sea of activity. Thousands of birds were streaming in from every direction. They had returned from battle and were anxious to receive their next assignments.

The lights on the stage came on. Whiteface waddled out. The air was filled with shrieking and chirps and whistles and buzzes. Feathers flew everywhere.

Whiteface motioned everyone to settle down. "Please," he said, "We are only part way to our destination."

I could hear a bird shouting, "What are we waiting for? Let's finish the job!"

Whiteface smiled. "All in good time," he said. "Tonight, we will celebrate the work you have done so far." He held up a copy of his book for everyone to see.

"As recorded in The Last Cycle, chapter six, page 86…" He turned to a marker in the book and started reading.

"A great bonfire shall mark the mid-way point. And on that bonfire, two humans in bird form shall be sacrificed. This will mark the beginning of the final chapter for all humans. And the creation of a world that welcomes only those creatures who have demonstrated their ability to adapt to their environment. A world dominated by birds."

Needless to say, the crowd went bananas. And I don't mean in a good way. Judy and I shuddered. The shrieks and caws were deafening. Some of the lights on stage swiveled around so they pointed directly at us. It was blinding. And it caught both of us by surprise.

"Now," Whiteface shouted, "as the sacred text says, bring us two volunteers." Volunteers? Judy and I never volunteered for anything. And we certainly would never volunteer to sacrifice ourselves for anything. But before we had a chance to object, the penguins were already lifting up the side of our cages.

They took us by the wings, one on each side, and escorted us through the crowd to the front of the stage. I tried to shake free at one point, but it was impossible. The penguins had super-heavy bodies and an ultra-strong grip.

Before we knew it, Judy and I were positioned alongside the bonfire on opposite sides of the tent-like structure. The penguins used string that had been wound together to lash us against the bamboo poles. I called out to Judy,

"Judy, can you hear me?"

Judy said yes.

"We're going to get out of this," I said.

"I know we are," she said.

I could tell from her trembling voice that she didn't believe it. But I did. I may be a sucker for things like destiny and fate. But I could feel in my little bird bones that we weren't finished yet. I just hoped those feelings were right. Otherwise, they'd be the last feelings I ever had.

Mr Crane approached, carrying the 'box of fire'. He set it down and opened up a lid on top. He then pushed a stick down inside of it that had one end tied up with a bunch of leaves and string. The stick caught fire immediately. He signaled over to Whiteface that he was ready to light the bonfire.

"Birds of the world," Whiteface shouted, "for your bravery and courage, for all that you have done so far, and all that you are about to do, let this sacrifice begin!"

Mr Crane started moving toward us. I shouted at the crowd. "Listen to me! We didn't volunteer for this! And there's no such thing as a sacred text. It doesn't exist!"

There was a confused murmur in the crowd. Mr Crane hesitated. Whiteface was furious. "Do it now!" he yelled. "Light the bonfire!" Mr Crane turned back to us. He pushed the flame into the stack of dried twigs and leaves.

Suddenly, there was a loud 'CLUNK' and the stick fell from his grasp. He looked confused. He picked it up again and was just about to light the bonfire a second time when... 'CLUNK', he dropped the stick a second time.

Whiteface shouted at him, "What is wrong with you? Here, give me that!" Whiteface scurried over.

He bent down to pick up the burning stick when 'WHAM!', he was hit in the head by a rock.

He looked up. Another rock hit him square in the forehead. "Oww!" he cried.

A fifth rock clobbered Mr Crane on the top of his head. He scurried away in a panic.

There were five rocks on the stage now, all of them lying close to each other. Whiteface looked confused. Each of the rocks had a thin piece of paper tied around them. He glared at the crowd.

"All right, who did this? WHO DID THIS?!"

The crowd was silent. They were terrified. From where Judy was standing, she couldn't see the rocks. But I could. And I knew exactly where they came from.

"Why don't you read what's on them," I said.

Whiteface spun around. "What?"

I said, "It looks like there's some kind of a message on each of them. Why don't you read what it says?"

Whiteface was furious. "You are the sacrifice," he said. "Sacrifices are not supposed to say anything."

"Well, this one is. So, what are you going to do about it?"

Whiteface looked over at the burning stick. It had gone out. He grunted with frustration.

"I'll show you what I'm going to do about it." He picked up the stick and put it back into the burning box.

"Or maybe you're a chicken!" I said. Just loud enough so that everyone could hear.

Now, I don't usually say bad things about chickens or any other creatures for that matter. And there weren't a lot of chickens in the crowd anyway, since most of them were still locked up in their cages, and the ones that did get free had a hard time getting here because they couldn't fly. So, to all of you chickens out there, I apologize. And I'll probably end up coming back as a chicken in the next life, if there is such a thing. But I had this idea, and it's the only one that I had, and I thought Whiteface might go for it.

"Cluck, cluck, cluck," I said, baiting him further.

Whiteface froze. "Are you calling me a chicken?"

"Well, if you're not a chicken, then you must be a scaredy-cat."

"I'm no chicken and I'm no cat. And I'm not afraid of anything. Especially you," he said.

"Then how come you're afraid to read the message on those rocks?" I said.

Judy heard what I was saying. She said, "Yeah, Mr Whiteface, what are you afraid of?"

At that point, someone from the crowd shouted, "Read the message, mate. What does it say?" Whomever it was had a foreign accent and sounded a lot like Tewksbury. And then I was pretty sure that I heard the two woodpeckers starting a chorus of, "Read the message! Read the message!"

Whiteface had heard enough. The crowd was restless. And the idea of him being afraid was starting to spread.

Whiteface scowled. He knew the only way to stop it was to read one of the messages that the carrier pigeons had brought.

"Mr Crane, hand me one of those rocks."

Chapter 37

The Unravelling

Mr Crane picked up one of the rocks from the stage floor. He cut the string that was holding the message in place and handed it to Whiteface.

Whiteface unfolded the message and read it. His white face turned red.

"Hand me a different one." He motioned for Mr Crane to hand him one of the other rocks. Mr Crane did as he asked.

Whiteface unfolded that message and read it. His face turned even redder. He was furious now.

"Give me the other ones," he said.

Mr Crane picked up the rest of the rocks and removed the messages. He handed them, one by one, to Whiteface.

Whiteface quickly scanned them and then crumpled them up and threw them to the ground. He glared over at me. "Is this some kind of a joke," he said.

I shrugged. I had no idea what he was talking about because I hadn't read the messages. But I could guess.

I guessed that my brothers had come through. That they had found the Oct. 13, 2011 dishwasher advertisement that was the basis for Whiteface's entire book. And that all I had to do was prove it to the crowd.

"Whatever your plan is, it won't work," he said. "And it won't save you. You're still going to be sacrificed."

He grabbed the flaming stick from the firebox and waddled toward me. His eyes were bright red, reflecting the flame as he bent down to light the bonfire.

Just then, a small black shadow appeared overhead, swooping majestically down over the stage. It was Old Crow. And he was holding something in his beak.

It was a piece of old, yellowed newspaper. It flapped in the wind as he landed and dropped it onto the ground.

I could see that it was the 'sacred text'. Mr Crane saw the paper and went ballistic. "Ahhh! What are you doing!" He came running out onto the stage but tripped and landed right at Whiteface's feet.

"What are you doing?" Whiteface said, looking down at him. Mr Crane looked up at him in horror. "That's the sacred text!" he said. "That old crow had it in his mouth."

Whiteface didn't seem particularly troubled by that fact. "So, go take it from him," Whiteface ordered.

Mr Crane crawled across the stage toward Old Crow to pick up the paper but Old Crow pulled it away at the last second.

Old Crow then flew up and placed the 'sacred text' face down onto the ice screen so that everyone in the crowd could see it. He then turned to me with a smile.

"What shall we do next, oh, wise one?"

I smiled back. "Let's place one of those rock messages alongside it and compare," I said.

Old Crow picked up one of the messages from the ground and placed it, face down, next to the sacred text on the ice-projecting screen.

"Oh, no, you don't!" Whiteface made a lunge for the sacred text but Old Crow raised one up of his feet and tripped him. Whiteface crashed headfirst onto the stage.

As soon as the two images appeared side by side on the screen, a murmur ran through the crowd.

"What are we looking at here, Mr Thrasher?" Old Crow knew very well what we were looking at. But he also understood that it wasn't going to be easy for others in the crowd to follow what I was about to say.

I knew that I had to use my loudest voice. "On the left side is the so-called 'sacred text' that Whiteface has been using to justify his war against the humans", I shouted out.

"On the right side is an advertisement for a dishwasher that my brothers found on the internet. They are the same message," I said, "Only Whiteface as changed some of the words to trick you."

The crowd looked confused. Whiteface stood up and addressed the crowd. "He's lying," Whiteface said, "That is an ancient text that predicts the future."

"It is a newspaper advertisement for dishwashers," I said. "The only thing Whiteface has done is cross out some of the advertiser's words and substitute his own. There is no sacred text. And Whiteface is no leader. He's a con artist. A crook!"

No one in the crowd knew what a con artist was. And most of them didn't know what the internet was either, but it didn't matter. Because they were starting to doubt his authenticity.

Someone shouted, "You mean, we've been hoodwinked?"

Whiteface pushed Old Crow aside. "Listen to me!" he shouted, "These two are the fakers. They're the con artists. The sacred text is authentic. Everything in my book is true. Humans can't adapt. All they know how to do is pollute the skies and water. And they're doing it to get rid of us birds!"

A voice shouted out, "Prove it!" It was Tewksbury. He pushed his way to the front of the crowd and stood just below the stage, looking up. "Prove it, and we'll follow you."

Whiteface blinked. And said nothing. He was like a deer caught in headlights. He'd just frozen.

"He can't," I said. "Because it's not true. Humans don't want to get rid of birds because they know that, if they do, it means that it's all over for them too. Besides, they like birds. They're our friends."

Old Crow chimed in, "He's right. I've never known humans to be the enemy of birds."

"Except when they eat you!" Whiteface shouted.

"That's true," I admitted. "Humans do eat birds. They shouldn't and most of them know it. They can live off plants. But that's not the point. The point is, humans are trying to change. They are trying to adapt. They are trying to make less smoke and less heat. They're doing everything they can because they know that time is running out, and if they don't, it will all be over."

My words just hung there in the cold northern air. I didn't realize how quiet the crowd had become until I stopped talking. They had heard every word that I said.

I turned to Judy and whispered. "Hey, Judy? Are you still there?" A moment went by.

And then Judy said, "Yes. I'm here. That was really great."

"Why is it so quiet out there?" I whispered.

"They're thinking," she said. "At least I think they're thinking." She wasn't sure. "What do you think?"

I began to hear voices questioning Whiteface's authority. "Maybe this whole thing is a mistake," someone said.

"I mean, we barely even know this guy," another one said.

And then, from out of the blue, Old Crow had one more thing to say. "Birds of all feathers," he announced. "I have one last bit of information to share with you. It is something that I suspected all along."

He unrolled a piece of paper that he had hidden under his wing and placed it face down on the ice screen.

The crowd gasped. I could barely see the screen from where I was standing. But I could see it well enough to know what it was that Old Crow was showing them.

It was a photo of a tough-looking guy named Derek Whiteface. And beside him was a tall, beady-eyed fellow by the name of Jeffrey Crane.

I suddenly realized that these weren't just photos that we were looking at, they were mugshots. I'd seen others like them before on TV. They're taken at the police station just before criminals are sent to jail.

"Where did you get those?!" Whiteface howled. "Those were supposed to be private."

Well, now, there's private and then there's confidential. And then there's 'top secret' that almost nobody is supposed to see. And my guess is Whiteface was hoping that these particular photos would have remained top secret forever. But now that everybody has seen them, they weren't top secret any more, were they? And everybody who saw them now knew that Whiteface and Mr Crane used to be human.

For some reason, the crowd didn't seem to care. It didn't make much difference to them. But it did to me. That photo of Whiteface sent shivers up my spine. It had 'creepy' written all over it. Whiteface was glaring over at Mr Crane.

"You said you burned those!" Mr Crane hung his head in shame.

"I know. But it's the only pictures of us that I have from the old days. I had them hidden in my travel case. That despicable old crow must have found them."

Old Crow was grinning. "Hey, you can run but you can't hide," he said.

"Shut up, you old buzzard!" Whiteface yelled. "And speaking of old, why aren't you dead yet?"

Old Crow shrugged. "Because I'm not that old. There was this crow once that lived in New York State and he was sixty-nine years old and he was blind. And his owners…"

"Quiet! I don't want to hear about it," Whiteface cut him off. He turned to me. "So what? So, we were human too. We aren't any more and that's all that counts."

"Let me guess what happened," I said, "there was this big storm…"

"We were in prison," Whiteface said, "minding our own business, when this crazy bluebird flew into the exercise yard and crashed into one of the windows. Turns out, me and string bean over there," he pointed to Mr Crane, "had made the same wish at the same time, to become birds and fly out of there. Later that night, there was a storm. The following morning, bingo, we'd been turned into birds. We didn't hang around to figure out why. We just flew the coop."

"Later on," he said, "I dreamt up this 'defeat the humans' thing as a way to get back at everybody who had ever done us wrong. Which was basically everybody."

I couldn't believe it. Here were two guys who got a second chance at life and what did they do with it? They tried to rule the world. Why does everybody want to rule the world? Why can't they just meet somebody and be happy and enjoy what life has to offer?

"Well," I said, "looks like you've done a pretty good job of screwing things up."

I realized I'd stepped over the line with that comment. I mean, who was I to talk, strapped to a bunch of bamboo poles, about to be turned into a crispy critter?

"Only I'm not finished yet," Whiteface declared. "But you are. Mr Crane, call in the condors!"

Chapter 38

Into the Drink

Mr Crane stuck his beak in the air. He let out a blood curdling shriek that I'd never heard before.

A moment later, two giant Andean condors appeared. They circled down over the top of the stage. Then they dropped down and landed with a great flapping WHOOSH.

Mr Crane undid the lashes that were holding Judy and me to the bamboo poles. I was just about to fly off and escape when one of the condors sunk his talons deep into my feathery sides and lifted me skyward.

I struggled to get free but it was pointless. They were ten times bigger than me and really fast. Have you ever seen a condor? I mean, nothing can stop these guys. A moment later, I was a hundred feet in the air with the crowd below me.

I could see Judy off to the side, struggling to get loose. She got free at one point and started to fall. But then her condor swooped down and caught her again.

Within minutes, we were high above the surrounding hills and headed for the horizon. I could see water glistening in the distance. Labrador Sea water, which is about as cold as you can get without actually being frozen.

Back on stage, there was a great commotion. Whiteface was trying to calm the crowd down. "Look, forget these pictures," he said. "That was a long time ago. People change. The point is, we've come this far. We've got the humans on the run. Now we must go all the way and destroy them!"

But there was a small group of birds near the front who had different ideas. Tewksbury faced the crowd. "You know what? I don't believe these guys," he shouted. "I think they're crooks!"

Barry and Chip, the two woodpeckers on either side of him, agreed. "We know Thrasher and Wren," Barry said. "We've traveled with them. They're good birds."

Some of the younger birds seemed confused. They'd spent their whole lives believing in The Last Cycle. "Why should we believe you?" one of them shouted.

Tewksbury shouted back, "Because we've always been birds and they haven't. We've been around forever. We've thought for ourselves and supported each other. Why change now? Why should we follow these clowns instead of following our instincts?"

Whiteface didn't like it when Tewksbury used the word 'clown'. I mean, who would? Plus, he was smart enough not to play Tewksbury's game.

"Don't listen to him! Listen to me! It's all in my book. Chapter two. The first thing a human will say is, 'don't follow Whiteface', which is exactly the reason why you should! Because you can't trust them. I know humans. I used to be one. Believe me, they are doing everything they can to destroy us."

"You mean, you're doing everything you can to destroy us," Tewksbury said. "Humans have no reason to hurt us. Look at all the eggs the chickens have given them. We eat the mosquitoes they hate. They enjoy our songs. They watch us with binoculars because they think we're beautiful. They don't want to destroy us. They want to save us. They just don't know how."

Meanwhile, behind the stage, Old Crow had found Rio and was talking to him. "You've got to do something," he said, "Or the condors will kill your young friends."

Rio turned around to the five carrier pigeons who were just standing there with blank faces, listening. "What are you waiting for?" he said. "Go!" The pigeons took off at once.

One of them looked confused and called back, "Where are we going?"

Rio shouted, "Find the condors!"

If Old Crow hadn't talked to Rio right then, we'd have been goners, for sure. The condors had every intention of dunking Judy and me in the water for as long as it took, until we had no more bird breath left in us.

As the giant condors crossed the icy beach and headed out into the bay, Judy was right alongside me. I could tell from her expression that she was terrified. I was too. I remember thinking that this is probably the last time we'd see each other. And that everyone and everything we had ever known and done was about to vanish forever.

And then I had this random thought. You know how you get those kinds of thoughts at the weirdest times? I thought it must have been baffling to the prison guards when Whiteface and Mr Crane disappeared. One day, they're sitting in their prison cells locked down for the evening. And the next morning, they're just gone. I bet whoever was in charge of the prisoners that night got in big trouble.

And then I had this other thought: if I hadn't tried to cheat on that math test that day, and if Judy hadn't brought an apple to school, neither of us would have got a detention and we wouldn't be in this pickle. You see? There's that expression again. "In a pickle." I still didn't know where it came from. I only knew we were in one. And there was no getting out.

The two condors swooped down low over the freezing cold water. Mine dropped me in with a SPLASH! And then Judy's. I could hear her little body hit the water.

Now, normally, it's not a big deal for a bird to get dunked in the water. But this water was so cold that my brain went numb immediately. I couldn't tell if I was upside down or downside up. Until my head and beak popped out of the water. Thank heavens. I could breathe again!

Then I felt a giant THUD! One of the condors nailed me a good one on the top of my head with his talon. That sent me spinning and spiraling down into the water again.

When I looked up, I could see the top of the water was way above me. I was holding my breath and my feathers were puffed up with air. I was like a soaking wet puffball that was ten feet below the surface of the water.

I tried using my wings but they weren't working very well. I kicked my feet, but they weren't like human feet. They were these tiny sticks that hardly did anything.

The water was dark green all around me. I looked over. I could see another dark mass doing the same thing. I was sure it was Judy. We were both struggling to get back to the surface, fighting to hold our breath.

I must have been inches from the surface when I could feel my lungs giving out on me. I couldn't hold my breath any more. The cold had paralyzed all of my muscles.

I was starting to sink back down again. And I thought to myself, "Well, that's it. So much for old Roy. See you later. Adios. It's been a slice."

And then the weirdest thing happened. Two shadows appeared overhead. Four talons dipped down into the water and grabbed me by the wings and YANKED me out of the water.

It was the carrier pigeons. And who knows how much those guys can carry, but it took two of them to pull me out and they were struggling.

I looked over and two more had their talons around Judy's head and were pulling her out of the water. She didn't know whether to be more shocked from almost drowning or from being dragged headfirst out of the drink.

From my perspective, it's always better not to drown, no matter how you get rescued. You could probably put that on my tombstone and I wouldn't complain. "Here lies Roy, pulled from the water with no complaints!"

The four carrier pigeons did a magnificent job of taking us back to the mainland. The fifth carrier acted as a lookout, just in case the condors came back. Which they didn't. I guess they figured their job was done. And you can bet, if Whiteface or Mr Crane knew what had happened, they wouldn't have given them any compliments.

In less than twenty minutes, we were flying over the top of the circle of hills and down onto the flat land where the stage had been set up.

Chapter 39

Uprising

I could see that there was something happening below, a real commotion. Wings were flapping and feathers were flying. It was a major dust-up. And in the center of it all, was Tewksbury, Rio, and Old Crow, who looked as if they had managed to turn the crowd against Whiteface and Mr Crane.

As we got closer, I could see Whiteface and Mr Crane shouting at everyone, "Get back!" Whiteface yelled. "Don't you see what's going on here? I'm your savior! I'm here to help!"

Old Crow laughed. "The only thing you ever helped was yourself. And now, your time is up."

Mr Crane was fumbling around for the ice screen projector. He put up the picture of the cartoon humans and the birds and the big cloud of smoke between them. "Wait a minute. Remember all the smoke that humans have caused?"

He was right, of course. And the birds knew it. But it didn't mean that humans wanted to get rid of them. Two wrongs don't make a right.

"We're not idiots!" one of the birds shouted. "If we do what you say, not only will there be smoke, but there'll be fire as well!"

The crowd was definitely turning against them. "I've seen humans plant trees," someone shouted. "Lots of them."

"And people have bird feeders," another one said. "If they'd wanted to get rid of us, why would they do that?"

Mr Crane didn't have an answer. He kept pointing to the picture on the screen and mumbling to himself. "No, no. It's all here in black and white. You see, there's the smoke, and now here's the birds, and there's the smoke, and…"

Rio had heard enough. He pulled the plug on the screen. Mr Crane bellowed, "Hey! You can't do that!"

Rio said, "Oh, no? Then how come I just did it?"

Then Rio heard something that caused him to look up at the sky. "Well, now. Look what the cat dragged in."

The carrier pigeons were circling overhead. They dropped down, depositing Judy and me onto the stage, and then flew off. We got to our feet and shook ourselves off.

Whiteface was furious. "You again! What happened to the condors?!" He looked around.

The two condors were standing in the middle of crowd. They were head and shoulders above everyone else.

"Don't just stand there," Whiteface howled, "drown them!" One of the condors was casually cleaning his beak with a stick.

He stopped what he was doing and said, "Nope."

"What do you mean, 'Nope'?" Whiteface howled. "You have to do what I say!"

The other condor said, "Uh-uh. We've changed our minds." He looked over at Judy and me. "We're sorry we dropped you guys into the water. That was a big mistake."

"You can't just change your minds," Whiteface exclaimed. "What about The Last Cycle and the end of all humans?"

"We don't believe that stuff any more," the first condor said. "We have a much better idea."

Whiteface was livid. "Oh, YOU have a better idea. Well, tell me, Mr Smarty Pants, what is your BETTER idea?"

The two condors smiled at each other. Then leaped into the air. They flew across the crowd to where the two empty bamboo bird cages were still standing. The ones that held Judy and me.

Each condor picked up one of the cages and flew it back across the crowd.

The first condor dropped his cage right on top of Whiteface with a THUD. The second one dropped his cage over Mr Crane. The two birds HOWLED. "Hey! Let us out!"

Seconds later, Rio and Old Crow lashed the two bird cages to the floor of the stage so they couldn't escape.

Old Crow turned to Judy and me. He smiled. "Roy Thrasher and Judy Wren, it's time for you to tell everyone your plan."

Instantly, the crowd went quiet.

Now, I've been put on the spot before. Like the time when I said that I'd finished my essay on the early explorers, but I hadn't even started it and the teacher asked me to stand up in front of the class and read it out loud. But that was nothing compared to this. This felt like the fate of the world was in my hands. Or wings. Whatever.

I knew I couldn't come up empty. Or say something that wasn't true. They'd know it, for sure. But maybe I didn't have to. Maybe what I had to say was already inside of me and all I had to do was uncover it.

I stepped forward. I didn't know what I was going to say even up until when I stood at the ice microphone. But it didn't bother me for some reason. Even so, I still had a hard time coming up with the first words.

Chapter 40

The Plan

"Thanks for coming," I said.

Wow. Now there's a dynamite line. Who hasn't heard that one before? That's what the dentist says when you're on your way out the door. Or the fast-food guy behind the counter.

The crowd looked puzzled. They turned to each other. I glanced over at Judy. I could tell she was worried too. But I wasn't. I smiled. And took my time. I was in no hurry. It was all there inside of me. Just waiting to come out.

"You have no reason to listen to me," I said. "You know what I am. You know what Judy and I both are. We're humans. We may look like birds but we're not."

There were no catcalls or shouting. Nobody yelled at us to get off the stage. Even Whiteface and Mr Crane had gone quiet.

"We were brought here as part of an elaborate scheme to destroy all humans. So that birds could finally take their rightful place at the top of the pecking order."

Some of the crowd liked hearing that and some of them didn't.

"Now, maybe birds are better custodians of this planet than humans are. But we were all born here. And we all live here. And it's all any of us have got. So, we have a responsibility to look after it."

I liked using that word, 'custodian'. The janitor at our school had it written on a plaque on the desk in his office. I remember looking the word up and finding out that it meant, 'a person who has responsibility for or looks after something'. He was there to look after the school and he took responsibility for it. That made sense to me.

"Humans have created a lot of smoke and heat but none of us feel good about it. We have been reckless and irresponsible but we wished we weren't. When we get together, we talk about saving the planet, we don't talk about wanting to destroy it."

From somewhere at the back of the crowd, a tiny voice, "So why aren't you doing something about it?"

"We're trying," I replied, "But we're in a pickle and we know it." There, I said it. My dad would have been proud. "The problem is up here." I pointed to my head.

"Humans are not much different than you are. They need food and water and a safe place to rest their heads at night. But some of us are confused. Some of us think that if you get more stuff than you need it will make you happy. But sooner or later, they find out all that stuff doesn't make you happy, it just makes you exhausted. And that the only thing that brings real happiness are friends and family. We're not stupid. We know this stuff. Just like you do."

Again, from the back of the crowd, that same tiny voice called out, "So why don't you do something about it?"

I finally figured out who it was that kept saying that. It was Rio. I could barely see him. I smiled when I realized who it was.

"Why don't we do something about it? Good question."

I didn't have the answer to it. I only had what I thought. "We should. But a lot of times we're lazy and self-centered. We think the world is here to serve us. And there are other times when we figure, what's the point of doing anything because we're just going to die."

"So, what is the point?" Rio said.

"The point is that all of us are lucky to be alive even for an instant and we should appreciate that," I said. "And since we all want to be happy, we should help each other. And that's what Judy and I are going to do."

"Oh yeah? How are you going to do that?" Rio shouted.

I have to admit Rio was starting to get on my nerves. But I understood what he was trying to do and I appreciated it.

"We're going to leave here and spend the rest of our lives showing humans how to adapt to this planet. We're going to show them that helping all of the creatures of this world is the only way for all of us to be happy. That's what we're going to do. That's my plan."

I looked over at Judy. She seemed okay with that. The crowd was silent. I couldn't tell what they were thinking.

Rio considered what I had said. He shrugged. "That's good enough for me." He looked at some of the birds around him. "Is that good enough for you guys?" There was a long pause. They were thinking about what I had said as well. A few of them nodded. Then a lot of them.

"Yeah," a young chickadee said, surprised at the sound of her own voice. "That's good enough for me."

The birds started flapping their wings in approval. Soon, the air was filled with shrieking and cawing and loose feathers.

Old Crow was smiling. He knew I had the right words inside of me all along.

Whiteface was furious. "That's never going to work," he yelled. "You could be lying. You'll never get away with this!"

Mr Crane was clucking something about how Judy and I 'should never have been allowed to leave that detention' and that 'the human school system was no good anyway'.

Their voices were eventually drowned out by the applauding crowd. And soon, all I could see was them pushing and pulling at the bars of their cages trying to get free.

Chapter 41

Someone Calls Me 'Sir'

The birds hung around for a little while longer and then they started to take off. First, the pelicans and the storks flew up into the air and disappeared over the circle of hills. They had thousands of miles to go to get back to Africa and they wanted to catch as much of the remaining daylight as possible.

And then the Europeans left. There were millions of them, filling the sky with their flapping wings and beaks. Sparrowhawks, eagles, buzzards, harriers. They'd probably stop off in Iceland to rest up and feed themselves.

By the time the North and South American birds had gone, the flat plain inside the circle of hills felt empty. There was a ton of bird poop remaining, of course, but the air was not as cold any more, and pretty soon, the rains would come anyway and wash it all away.

After a while, there was nothing left but a few stragglers. Oddballs who had come late or had gotten lost or who just wanted to hang around and talk to Judy and me about what it was like to be human and how we were going to help the birds.

Tewksbury and the two woodpeckers asked me to sing a couple of songs before they left. They wanted me to come up with something original to celebrate what had just happened. But I couldn't think of anything, and frankly, I was exhausted.

I don't know how many of you have ever given a big speech before, but let me tell you, when you're done, all you want to do is go to sleep or go eat at some fast-food restaurant. I told Tewksbury to write down where he lived. Judy and I could come and visit him on the coast someday.

We knew we'd see the two woodpeckers again, for sure. They didn't live more than a couple dozen miles from us, just over the mountains. Judy and I promised to pay them a visit if we ever took a summer vacation together.

And then it was time to say goodbye to Rio and Old Crow. Which was sad because Old Crow was so old, and we didn't know if we'd ever see him again. He told us he was in his late twenties and that there had been this crow once in New York state that lived to be sixty-nine years old. I liked hearing that story because it meant there was a chance that we'd see him again.

Rio said we didn't have to say goodbye because we lived in the same 'hood'. We'd be running into each other all the time, whether we liked it or not.

Once they were gone, there was just Judy and me. And these two losers who were still stuck in their bird cages. You know who I'm talking about. I don't mind calling them losers because that's what they were. Anybody who gets a second chance at life and blows it like they did has got to be a loser.

I wanted to talk to them before we left. I walked up to Whiteface's cage and just stood there looking at him.

"I don't get it," I said. "Why did you want to take over the world?" I think he'd watched too many bad action movies when he was growing up, because he just grinned at me and said,

"Because it's take-over-able."

I was about to suggest that the next movie he watch be "The Sound of Music", but I decided to talk to Mr Crane instead. He was leaning against the bars of his cage, staring at something on the ground. It was a bug.

I had to know how he got mixed up with Whiteface. At first, Mr Crane didn't want to talk about it. And then he said that they'd been friends for a long time. Ever since they went to the same elementary school together. He said that Whiteface had started a gang once called, "The Whiteface Boys" and that Mr Crane had joined it because he thought it was cool.

I asked him, "What made his gang so cool?" Mr Crane said the gang had secret codes for everything. Like "86" meant, let's get rid of this guy and "Roger Wilco" meant, 'Got it, no problem' and "brain-surf" meant, stealing somebody else's ideas. I didn't bother asking him what makes a successful gang leader. I wasn't planning to start a gang any more since the first one I started didn't turn out very well.

I stepped back and looked at them both. They looked sad and pathetic in their bamboo cages. Mr Crane was smart. He could have done anything. But he probably felt like he was a nerd who could never get a girlfriend on his own so he joined up with Whiteface.

I could tell that Judy wanted to get going. I joined up with her and we started to walk away. We both knew what would happen next. "Hey!" Whiteface called out. "You can't just leave us here? We'll starve to death."

Judy and I kept walking. We wanted to hear him wail a bit more. "Come back! Please! I promise to be good. I'll even help out these dumb birds!"

Mr Crane told him to be quiet. Nobody wants help from a loser like him. "Who are you calling a loser?" Whiteface barked. "Besides, it takes one to know one."

"Aha!" Mr Crane said. "So, you admit you're a loser!" Whiteface denied saying that. "Yes, you did", Mr Crane insisted.

"No, I didn't," Whiteface called back. And they went on like this for a while. Until Judy and I couldn't take it any more. I spun around. And they both went quiet.

"If we let you go," I said, "you both have to promise that you'll do only good things from here on in. And I'll let all of the other birds know about your promise and they'll hold you to it."

The two of them thought about it for a moment. And then nodded solemnly. I started walking back toward their cages.

"And I don't ever want to see either of you again, do you understand?" They both nodded emphatically.

"Yes, sir," Mr Crane said.

I had to laugh. Inside, of course. Because nobody had ever called me 'sir' in my entire life. And to have it come from Mr Crane, our substitute teacher from hell, well, that just made it all that much sweeter!

I untied the lashing from the bamboo at the bottom of Mr Crane's cage and he climbed out. Within seconds, he was gone.

A moment later, I did the same thing with Whiteface and he took off as well, without even a thank you.

"Hey," he yelled after Mr Crane. "Wait up!"

Mr Crane shouted back at him, "Keep away from me!"

Whiteface said, "Don't be a loser!"

Mr Crane said, "You're the loser!" They went on like that until their voices trailed off.

"No, you're the loser!"

"No, you are!"

"No, you are!"

"You are!"

"You are!"

I was happy when I couldn't hear them any more. And then it was just Judy and I left. She leaned over and gave me a kiss. I was stunned.

She said, "Let's go." A moment later, the two of us took off for home.

Chapter 42

The Long Way Home

I didn't think it would take long to get back home but I was wrong. We weren't homing pigeons, so the route that we'd taken to get here wasn't etched in our tiny brains. Plus, even though winter was on its way out, it wasn't completely gone yet.

As we reached the mountains, the weather turned bad. The snow was coming down hard and we could barely see.

Judy and I set down somewhere near a lake and took shelter halfway up a tree. The snow kept falling for three days. There must have been five feet of it. We were hungry and cold. Plus, we didn't know where we were, which only made things worse. I remember thinking, "Here we go, saving the world, and we can't even get back home to tell anybody about it." But then I thought, it wouldn't have made much difference anyway because we were still birds.

When the snow finally stopped, everything looked different. The mountains appeared smaller somehow. The trees shorter. The rivers and creeks we had used as markers on the way up weren't visible any more. I brought out Old Crow's map but I didn't recognize anything.

We were lost. But we didn't panic. We'd been in this situation before. What my dad used to say about staying in one spot was true. You can think more clearly when you're not moving around all the time, plus others could find you. That is, if anyone was looking for you.

We could see the sun behind the clouds and which way it was moving. It had risen in the east and was going to set in the west. Since we were in the northern hemisphere, if we stood facing the sun, then the east would be on our left and the west would be on our right. Right?

We knew we wanted to travel southwest, so it was pretty easy to know which way to go. Eventually, we were going to run into the Crow's Nest Pass. And once we were in the pass, there was only one way to go.

We knew how to find food and water. When to rest. And how to keep safe from animals. It just took time, that's all. Time and patience. That was the key.

I was in no hurry. I loved being with Judy. We flew well together. We had a lot of the same thoughts. It was like we were meant to be together. Hard to believe, after all these years and all that time ignoring each other in the school hallways. That was the problem back then. We both had the same thoughts, only they weren't good ones.

But now, there we were. The only two creatures in sight, moving together with the same goal in mind. As far as I was concerned, I didn't want anything else. I was in no hurry to get home. I just liked being right here, now.

A few days later, we found the entrance to the Crow's Nest Pass. Our climb over the mountains was exhausting.

One day, we found a dead coyote next to a riverbank and ate some of it until a bear came along. That gave us lots of energy to travel the rest of the way through the pass.

Once out of the mountains, it was easy to find our way over the high plateau. The further south we traveled, the warmer the weather got. I think it was spring, but I wasn't sure. I couldn't remember the seasons or even what month it was. It didn't seem to matter that much.

A final stretch of hills lay before us. I recognized them immediately. I knew that just over that last one was the city. Where we had come from. And where our families were waiting for us. At least, I hoped they were.

It was a scary thought. Not because I was afraid they'd forgotten about us. They must have known we were still alive because my brothers had sent that message back.

It's just that we'd both changed so much. We weren't the same Judy and Roy that we were before. But things are always changing, aren't they? We wish they'd stay the same but they don't. Just look around. Is there anything here that is exactly the same as it was yesterday?

Right about then, I started to worry about what lay ahead for Judy and me. How were we going to handle our changes? How were we going to live as birds in the city? Would we even want to stay there?

As we rose up over the last hill, the downtown high rises came into view. Judy and I looked at each other. I could tell that she was nervous. So was I. I wanted to say something to make her feel better but I couldn't think of much.

"It's okay if you're feeling what I'm feeling," I said. "At least we're feeling it together."

As we came down over the harbor, I could see other birds flying below us. Seagulls, herons, crows. They were all returning to their regular lives, so why shouldn't we?

Well, the answer was obvious: we weren't humans any more. But we weren't entirely birds either. At least, it felt that way. So, what were we? Who knew? And what was going to happen to us? Nobody knew that either.

Once over the harbor, Judy and I flew across the city. The lights were on in the buildings below, so that was a good thing. At least the birds hadn't completely ruined the electrical system. The humans were able to fix what had been destroyed. Buses were running. The cars were backed up on the freeway as usual. It all looked pretty much as I remembered it.

We followed Main Street all the way up the hill. I could see Hummingbird Elementary School lying ahead of us on 41st Avenue. I could see kids kicking a soccer ball around out on the playing field. And a yellow school bus full of students closing its doors, as if getting ready to leave on a field trip.

I looked at Judy. "Your place or mine?" I asked her.

"Yours," she said. "I'm not ready to go home yet."

We flew over all of the neighborhood houses that I'd grown up with. That I knew so well. And a moment later, my house came into view. Have you ever been on a long trip and then come home and you have a feeling that none of this belongs to you? That maybe it used to, but it doesn't any more. Well, that's how I felt.

Chapter 43

The Tree of Life

Judy and I flew into the tall tree that sits on the boulevard just outside our house. I'd always thought that it was an elm tree but Judy seemed to think it was an ash. I never knew the names of trees, but all of a sudden, what kind of tree this was seemed important. Why? Because I was going to have to live in it from here on in.

Well, not forever. I mean, I could live pretty much anywhere. Just not in my house. As far as my parents and brothers knew, if I was still alive, I was probably being held prisoner by five carrier pigeons.

Judy and I sat together for a while in the tree. Finally, I said, "Well, this is it. This is our life." Back to making brilliant comments. At least that hadn't changed.

"At least we have a life," she said. "There were so many times when I thought we were finished."

I heard a car coming down the road. I could see that it was my dad. He turned into the driveway right below us.

A moment later, he got out carrying a briefcase and walked into the house. The door closed behind him.

"Was that your dad?" Judy asked. I nodded. "He looks like an okay guy," she said.

"He is an okay guy," I said. "I mean, there are worse things you can say about someone."

"You want to look in through the windows?" Judy asked. I shook my head. I knew my two brothers would be home. And my mom would be in the kitchen starting dinner.

"You mind if I check out my place?" Judy asked.

"I think I'll just stay here," I said. "I've probably seen enough for now." She could tell I was feeling sad. Part of me wanted to be alone. I had a lot of thinking to do. If I was going to spend the rest of my life as a bird, I'd better get used to it. 'Get busy living or get busy dying,' Isn't that a line from some movie?[1]

Judy said she'd be back later. "You know where to find me," I said, trying to be cool.

The moment Judy flew off, I got this bad feeling in my stomach. Like what if I never saw her again? I knew that was crazy because her parents didn't live that far away. I could go see her any time. She probably needed to be alone, like me. Both of us had a lot of thinking to do.

I was wrong about two things. Turns out both my brothers weren't home because Spencer came walking down the street about an hour later. I'm sure he'd been over at his girlfriend's place. I wanted to talk to him. I thought

---

[1] 'Shawshank Redemption: A Story from Different Seasons', a four-part novella by Stephen King, 1982

about flying down and pulling on his hair or something but what good was that going to do? He'd just get irritated and he might even try to clobber me.

And the second thing I was wrong about was when Judy was coming back. From where I was perched, I could just see this wooden clock we had on the mantlepiece above the fireplace. So, I knew when an hour had passed. And then two hours. And still Judy hadn't returned.

The sun went down and it got dark. Still, Judy hadn't returned. I was trying to remember her exact words. I think she said, "I'll see you later." I didn't want to bother her if she was feeling sad. We'd spent weeks together. Maybe she was sick of me. Who knows?

I watched the activity in my neighborhood. People coming and going. Lights turning on and off. It all looked just like I remembered it.

After dinner, my brother, Ryan, left with my dad. Ryan played dodgeball on Friday nights. He usually caught a lift with my dad who was going shopping. I could see Spencer in his room listening to music on the internet.

And there was my bedroom. Dark and empty. And then the lights came on, which totally surprised me. My mom was standing in the doorway, looking around. I could tell she was sad. I thought for a moment that she could see right out the window to where I was in the tree and she could see me. But then she turned the light off and closed the door.

An hour or so later, my dad came home with Ryan. They went inside and I could hear my dad lock the door. That was it. Everyone was in for the night. Except me.

That was probably the longest night I'd ever spent in my life. I wasn't going to bother Judy. No way. She said she'd be back and I believed her. And there's no way I could have connected with any of my family. Even if I had managed to ring the doorbell, they would have come out and seen what? Some stupid-looking bird staring at them?

I just sat there in that tree. Alone. If you've ever wondered whether birds can feel lonely sometimes, I assure you they can. And believe me, it's not a nice feeling.

Halfway through the night, it started to rain. And not just a regular rain, but a downpour. Judy and I had been through just about every kind of weather there was, but this rain felt particularly cold and nasty.

Around eleven pm, only one light remained on in the house. It was upstairs in my parent's bedroom. They were probably brushing their teeth and talking about what they were going to do tomorrow. And then that light went off.

I was left with darkness. Just the shapes of the houses on the block through the rain.

I could see the odd bird flying around. Who knew what they were up to? They were back to living their own lives. And after everything that happened with Whiteface and Mr Crane, they probably just wanted to be by themselves.

It must have been around two a.m. when the thunderstorm hit. Usually, if it's been raining out already, you don't get a thunderstorm as well. But this was different. The sky was totally black. I remember wishing I could be in my bed. All cozy and dry. And then I'd go to school like I always did. And then the world would make sense.

The first crack of thunder woke me up. That's how I knew I'd been asleep. I wasn't totally awake when I looked over and saw the shape of a bird sitting next to me.

At first, I thought it was Judy, but then I realized it wasn't. It was a blackbird. Or at least it looked black. I couldn't tell entirely. Maybe it was blue.

There was a flash of lightning that lit up his face. He was grinning. He looked kind of weird and beat up and the feathers on top of his head were all over the place.

When the lightning disappeared, so did he. I couldn't tell if I had dreamt him or not. Maybe I was so lonely I was imagining things. I reached out with my wing and felt where he had been standing but there was nothing there. So, I gave up and closed my eyes. And went back to sleep.

Chapter 44

Time to Wake Up

I woke up to the sound of a car being started. It was one of the neighbors. Their car slowly backed out in the street and then drove away. The sun was just starting to come up. Its rays were blinding. That's how I knew the clouds and the storm were gone.

I didn't feel like doing much. My first thought, of course, was about Judy. I figured I'd better head over to her place and see what happened.

But when I went to take off, something horrible happened. My wings didn't work. I felt paralyzed. In fact, I couldn't see my wings at all.

I flapped and flapped but nothing happened. All I could see were these two giant sausage-shaped things hanging from my shoulders. I leaned forward and almost fell out of the tree.

Yikes! I was twenty feet up with the sidewalk below me. And there were my scrawny legs dangling underneath.

I was freezing cold. I looked at the rest of my body. I had no clothes on. There was my chest and my knees and my elbows and my hands and everything else, all just hanging out there.

I heard the front door of our house close. It was Spencer, on his way to school. He must have been going to early morning band practice because he was carrying a trumpet case. As he came down the sidewalk, right underneath me, I gave out a scream.

"Spencer!"

Spencer stopped and looked around.

"Up here!" I shouted. "In the tree!"

Spencer looked up at me. His jaw fell open. He dropped his trumpet case.

"Roy?"

"I can't get down! I'm stuck up here!"

"Jesus, you're butt naked!" Spencer said.

"I know I'm butt naked! Get Dad! We're going to need the fire department. Hurry up!"

Spencer turned around and ran back into the house. I could hear him shouting at the top of his lungs.

"Dad! You've got to come out here! It's Roy! He's stuck up in a tree!"

And then I heard my dad's voice, "What tree? What are you talking about?"

Within minutes, a fire department truck and two medical emergency vehicles arrived.

The fire department guys sent up a ladder. One of them, this big smiley guy with a beard who was dressed in a rescue jacket, wrapped a blanket around me and escorted me down the ladder.

I remember him saying, "How the devil did you get up there?" and "Where are your clothes?" I didn't have any answers that would have satisfied him, so I kept repeating the same thing.

"I don't know. I just want to go home."

And that was just the beginning of things. All next week, the police and a bunch of social workers were at our house. My mom was a wreck. Well, she was happy but she was a wreck too. She told me they'd found Judy as well. Just minutes after they found me. She was also stuck up in a tree.

Man, I thought to myself, how embarrassing would that have been for Judy? Personally, I didn't care who saw me in the buff. I was just happy to be warm and dry and not freaking out all the time about getting eaten by some cat or a coyote.

My parents didn't let me talk to anybody for a few days. The social worker advised me to rest in bed and to just try and remember what had happened.

I could remember everything, of course, every detail, but that wasn't going to do me or them any good. What was I going to do? Tell them the 'blue bird of happiness' had turned me into a bird and that Judy and I had flown way up north to be a part of the Last Cycle of Humanity?

I thought it best to be mostly quiet and keep saying the same thing: "I don't remember. I wish I did, but I don't."

Eventually, the social workers left and the police cruiser that had been parked in the driveway left as well. My mom kept a close eye on me. She had told them that if

I suddenly remembered anything, she'd call them right away.

I kept asking my mom about Judy but she didn't seem to know anything. I asked her if I could call her on my cellphone but she said the police had taken it to the police station. She said I could use the house phone if I wanted.

I was still in my pajamas and slippers when I went downstairs to phone Judy. I got her parents' phone number from this school information sheet that my mom had tacked up on the kitchen bulletin board.

My mom listened from the hallway as I dialed Judy's phone number. I didn't care that she was listening. I just wanted to know if Judy was okay.

The phone rang a couple of times. I remember feeling anxious. It rang a third time. And then an answering machine came on. At first, it said, "We're sorry. The Wrens aren't home at the moment. Please leave a message and one of us will get back to you." And then it said, "I'm sorry, there is no more room for messages." And then it hung up.

Man, was that depressing! I looked at my mom in the hallway. She didn't have any expression. "You should probably head back to bed," she said. She had no idea how devastating that phone call was to me.

"I just wanted to know if she was okay," I said.

My mom smiled. "I know, honey. I'm sure you'll be able to talk to her soon."

I stayed home another three days before they let me go back to school. I guess it was a good thing my parents didn't let me watch the local news on TV. If I had, I would have seen the firemen helping me down the ladder with the blanket barely covering my butt and my scrawny legs.

But then I would have seen Judy being rescued as well. And that would have made all the difference in the world.

Chapter 45

Life Without Judy

The first day that I was supposed to go back to school I played hooky. At least for part of it.

My mom stood in the open doorway and watched me walk down the street. But as soon as I heard the door close, I did an about-face and headed off in the opposite direction.

I had to know what was going on with Judy and nothing was going to stop me.

She lived a few blocks away. I'd only been by her place a few times so I didn't know whether things looked normal or not. From the outside, it seemed really quiet. There were no lights on and the drapes were drawn shut.

I looked around to see if anyone was watching. Then I walked casually up to the front door and knocked as if I was a salesman or something. I waited for a while and then knocked again. Nothing. There was no sign of anything.

I looked in through the living room window. I could see through a space in the drapes that there was still furniture inside but that was about it. A few newspapers had been thrown into the bushes near the front door. I checked the dates. They were from a couple of days ago.

When I arrived at school, it was a really big deal. My homeroom teacher, Mrs Algonquin, made sure I was comfortable and asked me if I needed anything.

At recess, all the kids gathered around and demanded to know what had happened. I told them it was a mystery. That I don't really remember anything. They wanted to know why Judy hadn't returned to school. I said I didn't know. But that I really wanted to.

My so-called friend, Leonard, wanted to know if I'd been abducted by aliens. "Does your butt hurt?" he asked.

I said, "No more than usual."

I couldn't answer any of his or anybody else's questions because they would never have believed me. One girl thought that Judy and I were drug dealers who had tried out some weird drug and ended up in the trees. Once a rumor like that gets started, it's really hard to stop it.

I think the strangest thing of all is how people flock to you when they think that you're special or that you know things they don't know. Judy and I weren't special. We may have been through a lot, and changed a lot because of it, but underneath, we were the same people.

I had a hard time concentrating in my classes. All the ones that I used to share with Judy I just kept looking at her empty seat. And when I went out at recess or lunchtime, I wasn't able to listen to anyone who was talking to me. Nothing they said seemed important. And they mostly just wanted to know what the 'big mystery' was anyway.

One day, just before lunch, I asked Mrs Algonquin if I could go to the principal's office. She said that would be fine, but to hurry back.

The principal was this Norwegian guy named Mr Fiske. He reminded me of Mr Crane in that he was tall and thin and his hair stood out at the back of his head. But other than that, he was nowhere near as weird as Mr Crane.

I asked him if he had any idea where Judy was. He said he didn't know. He said Mr Wren had called him a few days ago. He said that the family would be going away for a while. But he never said for how long.

"I wouldn't be surprised," he said, "if they moved away for good after everything you two have been through."

I nodded politely. But his words hit me like a giant boulder in the stomach. Why hadn't Judy contacted me? She could have dropped by or called me at home. Anything, to let me know what was going on.

I wasn't sure how long I could hold things together. I felt like I was this ticking time bomb with all of these experiences and information and feelings inside of me and nobody to share them with.

The day after I talked to the principal, I told my mom that I wasn't feeling well and that I wanted to stay home. She said that was fine, whatever I needed.

But the only thing I needed was something that I couldn't get. She was gone. Moved away. Maybe forever.

My mind started to make up stories about what had happened. Maybe her parents thought I was a bad influence. Maybe Judy hadn't been truthful all along. Maybe, when she got turned into a bird, she figured the only way to survive was to just pretend that she liked me.

After a full day of thinking that kind of stuff, I felt like I was starting to go crazy. I told my mom that I wasn't feeling well and that it was probably better for me to take a couple of more days off school and she agreed.

The morning I went back to school again, my dad offered to give me a ride but I said no. I'd rather walk.

I left a few minutes early so that I could go by Judy's house again and see if anything had changed. I was trying not to appear like some creep who liked to look in through people's windows.

So, when I went by her house, I walked quickly, just glancing over long enough to get a quick look at the front door and the living room window.

The first thing I noticed was that the newspapers in the bushes were gone. And the drapes might have been moved just a bit. But I wasn't sure. Maybe I was just seeing things. But the newspapers were definitely gone. But then again, maybe it was just some neighbor that took them in order to tidy up.

I walked back and forth in front of the house twice. Finally, I gave up. I couldn't tell anything. And it was only making me more anxious. Plus, if I didn't hurry up, I was going to be late for school.

I have to say, those last few blocks on the way to school that day were the longest ones I have ever walked. I kept thinking this is probably going to be the way things are from here on in. Just me, walking to school, never knowing what happened to Judy, and listening to endless questions about what the two of us had been through.

Hummingbird Elementary has this parking lot that all of the teachers park in. And the way I walk to school, I usually go through the parking lot and in through the side door of the school. I guess it was a habit of mine to try and avoid talking to other students early in the morning.

Whatever it was, that's what I did that morning. And that's when something happened that would change my life again. And forever more.

I had my head down as I walked around some cars and so I didn't really see anything at first. And then I noticed a shape standing at the top of the stairs that lead into the side entrance to the school.

I remember thinking to myself, "This is the same place that Judy and I met after becoming birds. Right under those steps." I looked at the steps. They seemed so tiny and unimportant now. And I guess they are, to anyone but me.

And then I heard this voice coming from the top of the stairs. "Roy?" I looked up. I must have looked like a complete idiot because I froze and my eyes blinked and my jaw fell open.

It was Judy. I could not believe my eyes. "How come you didn't call me?" she said. I stood there in silence.

And then she said, "I'm sorry, I'm just joking. I know you must have tried to get hold of me. My grandmother got sick and we had to take a plane and go and see her right away. I texted you and emailed you but I didn't get a reply. I told my parents to try and get hold of you but they just didn't."

I was still in a state of shock. She smiled and came down the stairs and put her arms around me. "I missed you," she said. She had tears in her eyes.

I was starting to come back to reality. "Wow," I said, "I didn't think I was going to see you again."

"I know," she said, "I'm sorry."

"What happened to your grandmother?" I asked.

Judy moved her head back and forth. "She died."

I nodded. I didn't know what to say to that. People never know what to say when somebody tells them that somebody else died. So, they always end up saying, "I'm sorry." Which, I guess, isn't such a bad thing. I mean, you're not going to say, "Gee, I'll really miss those burritos that she used to cook" or "She really knew how to play the piano" because you don't know anything about her.

So, I just said, "I'm sorry." And that seemed to do the trick. Judy nodded and smiled.

"Wow," she said. "It is so great to see you. I guess we have a few things to talk about."

Now there was an understatement. Right then, the bell went off to signal the start of classes. We just looked at each other and smiled.

There was no way we were going inside.

Chapter 46

A Tale of Two Winners

Have you ever wished that you could see something just before it happened?

Well, there was this car once, an SUV. And it was travelling north on a highway called The Yellowhead. And it was winding its way along at a steady pace.

The people in the back seat of the car had a small box beside them that was filled with pieces of paper towel that had been torn up and formed into a kind of bed. And next to it was a little bowl of water that was half filled.

Inside the box was a tiny bird.

The car passed by a sign at the side of the road that said, "Spirit River" and then pulled off the highway.

The town was completely surrounded by mountains. They looked a lot like the mountains that were in The Crow's Nest Pass because, as it turns out, that wasn't very far away. It was also the reason that there was a veterinary clinic in town that was called, "The Old Crow Veterinary Hospital".

The car pulled into the gravel parking lot of the veterinary hospital and four people climbed out. There were two children and their parents.

The dad opened up the front door and the mom helped the two children carry the box up the stairs and inside.

A sign hanging down over the top of the counter inside said, "Please ring the bell for service." The dad rang the bell, and a moment later, a man came out from the back.

Now, I'm no genius. But something tells me you just might have an idea who that man was. No? Well, maybe I'll just tell you and get it over with.

It was me. Only I wasn't twelve years old any more. I was twenty-eight. And I was a lot bigger and I was wearing a surgical gown and had a face mask on the top of my head.

And then, from out of the back, came another person. And do you know who that was?

It was Judy. Only she wasn't on duty that day, so she was wearing regular clothes. She was a lot bigger too.

And a lot of things that kids have, like acne and big feet and ears that stick out, we didn't have that any more. And anybody who met Judy now would think she was beautiful. I know I did. I'd even heard that some people thought I was kind of good-looking but I never believed that. Time can take care of a lot of things but it can't change everything.

The family explained to Judy and me that they had been camping nearby and had found this bird lying on the ground near the washrooms. It looked like it needed water so they gave him some. And now they have brought him here to see what's wrong with him.

Judy and I took the tiny bird into the back where we could examine him. The family came with us. The kids looked really worried. It took me a while to examine the bird's eyes with a magnifying loupe and to check his pulse with my stethoscope. His heart was beating like crazy.

Something caught my attention and I looked up at Judy. I think she was seeing the same thing that I was seeing.

This was no ordinary bird. This was Rio. And he knew, and I knew, and Judy knew, that he didn't have much time left. That all things come to an end.

Even special creatures like him.

I looked at the family that had brought him in. I could tell that the parents knew the bird was a goner. And probably so did the kids. The little girl looked like she was going to cry. I told her that he was a very sick bird but that we'd do everything we could to save him.

That seemed to make her feel better. Her brother said they shouldn't hang around because they'd just get in the way, and the parents agreed.

On the way out the door, the parents thanked us for being so kind. Judy said we'll do what we can and that she hoped the rest of their camping trip went well. We watched them climb into their car and drive off.

Once they were gone, Judy and I went back into the examining room. We looked at the bird. He was old and barely breathing. His eyes were closed and they had a lot of gunk in them.

I wasn't certain about anything. So, I tried talking to him. I leaned over the examining table.

"Are you Rio?" I whispered. He didn't say anything. So, I tried again. "Are you Rio?" Nothing. I looked over at Judy. She shook her head. Maybe it wasn't.

I tried it one last time. "Are you…"

"Yes!" Rio blurted. "How many times are you going to ask?"

"Well, you didn't say anything," I said. "How was I supposed to know?"

"You're a doctor, aren't you?"

"I wasn't going to ask in front of those people," I said. "I'd look like a fruitcake."

Rio turned his head around. He was looking at Judy. "Well, look at you. You're all grown up," he said.

Judy smiled. "So are you," she said.

Rio shrugged. "I was grown up before," he said. "Now I'm just old. You can barely squeeze a dozen years out of one of these bodies. You should try it sometime."

We smiled. In a way, we had tried it. We'd both been there. Just not for very long.

I wanted to ask him something, but I wasn't sure if I was ready for the answer.

"What happened to Old Crow?" I said.

"You didn't hear?" Rio said. "I'm surprised. I figured somebody would have told you."

My heart sank. So did Judy's. I prepared myself for the bad news. But it never came.

"He's still around. I just saw him last week. He likes to go up into the Pass during the summer. He says you meet the nicest folks up there. Present company excluded, of course." Same old Rio.

"How old is he now?" I asked.

"He says he's forty," Rio said, "But nobody knows for sure. He's always going on about how he's going to break the world record and live to be seventy."

Rio looked tired. And his talking just seemed to make it worse. I suggested he get some rest and then we can see what we can do about his eyes. He thanked us and said he was glad those people had brought him here.

"You were right," Rio said. "Humans don't want to get rid of birds. They like us."

If you had been standing outside the hospital, you wouldn't have known what was going on inside. That Judy and I had talked to Rio and that he'd talked back to us.

And you wouldn't have known all of the things Judy and I went through in high school. If you'd seen us, you would have thought we were just some boyfriend and girlfriend. But it went a lot deeper than that. We were almost always together, and we didn't feel like losers any more because we'd learned to think for ourselves and to care about other people.

After high school, we went to university and took a lot of science courses and learned all about veterinary medicine. And then we got a loan from our parents and opened up this hospital. We loved what we did. It came naturally to us. And every day we woke up, we looked forward to helping whatever animals needed our care.

Rio lived another year at the hospital. Animals can live a long time when they don't have to worry about being eaten or getting sick.

As for Whiteface and Mr Crane, I heard they took off for South America and were never seen again. Given all that had happened, that was probably a good thing, since most birds wouldn't have treated them kindly anyway.

I forgot to mention, Judy and I got married two weeks after we graduated from university. A lot of people attended the ceremony, from both sides of the family, the Wrens and the Thrashers. I thought I saw the Bluebird of Happiness flying around that day but I couldn't be sure. I asked Judy if she had wished for something and she said no. She already had everything she could wish for. I think that was the best thing anybody ever said to me.

Well, that's it. That's my story. One moment, you feel like a total loser. The next moment, you're flying through the air with someone you love. Maybe not as a bird. Maybe just in an airplane. Who knows?

But the point is, everything changes all the time, so you want to be open to that. You want to take every opportunity that comes your way because you never know where it will take you.

And to all the Rios and the Old Crows and the Tewksbury's out there, I say, "Worm on!"